Welcome to the world of St Piran's Hospital

Next to the rugged shores of Penhally Bay
lies the picturesque Cornish town of St Piran,
where you'll find a bustling hospital famed
for the dedication, talent and passion
of its staff—on and off the wards!

Under the warmth of the Cornish sun,
Italian doctors, heart surgeons, and
playboy princes discover that romance blossoms
in the most unlikely of places…

You'll also meet the devilishly handsome
Dr Josh O'Hara and the beautiful,
fragile Megan Phillips…and discover the secret
that tore these star-crossed lovers apart.

*Turn the page to step into St Piran's—
where every drama has a dreamy doctor…
and a happy ending.*

Dear Reader

I am thrilled to be a part of the *St Piran's Hospital* continuity series, and have loved working alongside my favourite authors and being involved in such an exciting series.

My heroine Izzy is going through such a difficult time that my first instinct was to send in a hero that would fix everything for her—and, with a baby on the way, preferably fix things soon! I was delighted to find, though, that Diego had other ideas.

He's my ultimate sort of hero—he lets Izzy find her own solutions, trusts her perhaps more than she trusts herself, and is also incredibly sexy—I mean, *way* too sexy for a heroine who's sworn off men to deal with!

Happy reading!

Carol x

STOCKTON-ON-TEES BOROUGH LIBRARIES

dns0962.qxp

ST PIRAN'S: RESCUING PREGNANT CINDERELLA

BY
CAROL MARINELLI

MILLS & BOON

First published in Great Britain 2010
Harlequin Mills & Boon Limited,
Eton House, 18-24 Paradise Road, Richmond, Surrey TW9 1SR

© Harlequin Books S.A. 2010

Special thanks and acknowledgement are given to Carol Marinelli for her contribution to the *St Piran's Hospital* series

ISBN: 978 0 263 21524 3

Harlequin Mills & Boon policy is to use papers that are natural, renewable and recyclable products and made from wood grown in sustainable forests. The logging and manufacturing process conform to the legal environmental regulations of the country of origin.

Printed and bound in Great Britain
by CPI Antony Rowe, Chippenham, Wiltshire

Carol Marinelli recently filled in a form where she was asked for her job title, and was thrilled after all these years to be able to put down her answer as 'writer'. Then it asked what Carol did for relaxation. After chewing her pen for a moment Carol put down the truth—'writing'. The third question asked—'What are your hobbies?' Well, not wanting to look obsessed or, worse still, boring, she crossed the fingers on her free hand and answered 'swimming and tennis'. But, given that the chlorine in the pool does terrible things to her highlights, and the closest she's got to a tennis racket in the last couple of years is watching the Australian Open, I'm sure you can guess the real answer!

**Carol also writes for
Mills & Boon® Modern™ Romance**

ST PIRAN'S HOSPITAL
Where every drama has a dreamy doctor…
and a happy ending.

This December there's a real Christmas treat in store—
the first two St Piran's stories in one month!

Find out if Nick Tremayne and Kate Althorp
finally get their happy-ever-after in:
ST PIRAN'S: THE WEDDING OF THE YEAR
by Caroline Anderson

Then read on to see Dr Izzy Bailey be swept off her feet
by sexy Spaniard Diego Ramirez
ST PIRAN'S: RESCUING PREGNANT CINDERELLA
by Carol Marinelli

And there's plenty more romance
brewing in St Piran's!

The arrival of Italian neurosurgeon Giovanni Corezzi
will make you forget the cold in January
ST PIRAN'S: ITALIAN SURGEON, FORBIDDEN BRIDE
by Margaret McDonagh

Daredevil doc William MacNeil unexpectedly discovers that
he's a father in February
ST PIRAN'S: DAREDEVIL, DOCTOR…AND DAD!
by Anne Fraser

The new heart surgeon has everyone's pulses racing
in March
ST PIRAN'S: THE BROODING HEART SURGEON
by Alison Roberts

Fireman Tom Nicholson steals Flora Loveday's heart in April
ST PIRAN'S: THE FIREMAN AND NURSE LOVEDAY
by Kate Hardy

Newborn twins could just bring a May marriage miracle
for Brianna and Connor Taylor
ST PIRAN'S: TINY MIRACLE TWINS
by Maggie Kingsley

And playboy Prince Alessandro Cavalieri
comes to St Piran in June
ST PIRAN'S: PRINCE ON THE CHILDREN'S WARD
by Sarah Morgan

CHAPTER ONE

'I'M READY to come back to St Piran's.'

No words filled the silence, there was no quick response to her statement, so Izzy ploughed on, determined to make a good impression with Jess, the hospital counsellor. 'I'm really looking forward to being back at work.' Izzy's voice was upbeat. 'I know that a few people have suggested that I wait till the baby is born, I mean, given that I can only work for a couple of months, but I really think that this is the right thing for me.'

Still Jess said nothing, still Izzy argued to the silence. 'I'm ready to move on with my life. I've put the house on the market....' She felt as if she were at an interview, effectively she *was* at an interview. After the terrible events of four months ago, Ben Carter, the senior consultant in A and E, had told her to take all the time she needed before she came back to the unit where she worked as an emergency registrar.

It would have been far easier to not come back, and at nearly twenty-eight weeks pregnant she'd had every reason to put it off, but Izzy had finally taken the plunge, and instead of ringing Ben to tell him her decision, she had dropped by unannounced. But to her surprise, instead of welcoming her back with open arms, Ben had gently but firmly informed her that it would be *preferable* if she see one of the hospital counsellors.

'I'm fine!' Izzy had said. 'I don't need to see a counsellor.'

'You are seeing someone, though?' Ben had correctly interpreted the beat of silence.

'I was.' Izzy had swallowed. 'But I'm fine now.'

'Good!' Ben had clipped. 'Then you won't have a problem speaking with someone else.'

'Ben!' Izzy had hardly been able to contain her fury. 'It's been four months! You know me—'

'Izzy!' Ben had interrupted, refusing to be manipulated. 'I worked with you daily, I've been to your home, I got on well with Henry and yet I had no idea what you were going through, so, no, I'm not convinced I do know you or that you'd come to me if you had a problem.'

Izzy had sat with pursed lips. Ben could be so incredibly kind yet so incredibly tough too—he would let nothing jeopardise the safety of his patients or his staff and he was also completely honest and open, so open it actually hurt to hear it sometimes. 'I've spoken with my senior colleagues...'

'You've discussed me?'

'Of course,' Ben had replied. 'And we all agree that coming back to A and E after all you've been through is going to be tough, that we need to look out for you, and rather than us asking every five minutes if you're okay, which I know will drive you crazy, I'm going to insist that you see someone. I can page Jess Carmichael—she's good, all very informal, you can go for a walk, have a coffee...'

'I'm not sitting in the canteen, chatting about my life!' Izzy had bristled. 'I'll see her in her office.'

'Fine,' Ben had responded, and then his voice had softened. 'We want what's best for you Izzy.'

So here she was, on a Friday lunchtime, just before her first shift back, *again* sitting in a counsellor's office, telling the same thing to Jess that she had to Ben, to her mother, to her friends, that she was fine.

Fine!

'It's often suggested,' Jess said, when Izzy had told her that her house was on the market, 'that people wait twelve months after a bereavement before making any major life changes.'

'I'm twenty-eight weeks pregnant!' Izzy gave a tight smile. 'I'd suggest that change is coming whether I'm ready or not. Look...' She relented a touch because Jess was nothing other than nice. 'I don't want to bring the baby home to that house—there are just too many memories. I really want a new home by the time the baby comes.'

'I can understand that,' Jess said. 'Have you people to help you with moving?'

'Plenty,' Izzy said, 'Now I just need someone to make a half-decent offer on the house.'

'How will you feel—' Jess had a lovely soft Scottish accent, but her direct words hit a very raw spot '—when a domestic abuse case comes into the department?'

Izzy paused for a moment to show she was giving the question due thought then gave her carefully prepared answer, because she'd known this would be asked. 'The same as I'll feel if a pregnant woman comes into the department or a widow—I'll have empathy for them, but I'm certainly not going to be relating everything to myself.'

'How can you not? Izzy, you've been through the most awful experience,' Jess said and even her lilting voice couldn't soften the brutal facts. 'You tried to end a violent, abusive relationship to protect the child you are carrying, and your husband beat you and in his temper drove off and was killed. It's natural to feel—'

'You have no idea how I feel,' Izzy interrupted, doing her best to keep her voice even, a trip down memory lane was the last thing she needed today. 'I don't want the "poor Izzy" line and I don't want your absolution and for you to tell me that none of this was my fault.'

'I'm not trying to.'

'I've dealt with it,' Izzy said firmly. 'Yes, it was awful, yes, it's going to be hard facing everyone, but I'm ready for it. I'm ready to resume my life.'

Only Jess didn't seem so sure, Izzy could tell. She had made such an effort for this day—she was immaculately dressed in a grey shift dress with black leggings and black ballet pumps, her blonde short hair, teased into shape, and large silver earrings adding a sparkle to her complexion. She had been hoping to look every inch a modern professional woman, who just happened to be pregnant. She would not let Jess, let anyone, see behind the wall she had built around herself—it was the only way she knew to survive.

Jess gave her some coping strategies, practised deep

breathing with her, told her to reach out a bit more to friends and Izzy ran a hand through her gamine-cut blonde hair that had once been long and lush but which she'd cut in a fit of anger. Just when Izzy thought the session was over, Jess spoke again.

'Izzy, nothing can dictate what comes into Emergency, that's the nature of the job.' Jess paused for a moment before continuing. 'No matter what is going on in your life, no matter how difficult your world is right now, you have to be absolutely ready to face whatever comes through the doors. If you feel that you'd rather—'

'Are you going to recommend that I be sent to Outpatients?' Izzy challenged, her grey eyes glittering with tears that so desperately needed to be shed but had, for so long, been held back. 'Or perhaps I can do a couple of months doing staff immunisations—'

'Izzy—' Jess broke in but Izzy would not be silenced.

'I'm a good doctor. I would never compromise my patients' safety. If I didn't feel ready to face A and E, I wouldn't have come back.' She gave an incredulous laugh. 'Everyone seems to be waiting for me to fall apart.' She picked up her bag and headed for the door. 'Well, I'm sorry to disappoint you all, but I refuse to.'

Izzy was a good doctor, of that Jess had no doubt.

As she wrote her notes, she was confident, more than confident, that Izzy would do the right thing by her patients, that she was more than capable to be working in Emergency. But at what cost to herself? Jess thought, resting back in her chair and closing her eyes for a moment.

Jess wanted to send a memo to the universe to insist only gentle, easy patients graced Izzy's path for a little while.

Only life wasn't like.

Jess clicked on her pen and finished writing up her notes, worried for her client and wishing more progress had been made.

Izzy Bailey, while still fighting the most enormous private battle, was stepping straight back into the front line.

CHAPTER TWO

'OBSTETRIC Team to Emergency.'

Izzy heard the chimes as she tossed her coffee and sandwich wrapper in the bin and did a little dance at the sliding door that refused to acknowledge her, no matter how many times she swiped her card. An impatient nurse behind her took over, swiping her own card, and Izzy tailgated her in.

They'd start her in Section B.

Of that she was sure.

Writing up tetanus shots and suturing, examining ankles and wrists… Despite her assured words to Jess earlier, Izzy was actually hoping for a gentle start back and was quietly confident that Ben would have arranged for one.

'Obstetric team to Emergency.'

The chimes sounded again, but Izzy wasn't fazed. It was a fairly familiar call—frenzied fathers-to-be often lost their way and ended up bringing their wives to Emergency rather than Maternity.

Izzy glanced at her watch.

In ten minutes she'd be starting her first shift…

Walking through another set of sliding doors, which this time opened without the use of her card, Izzy found herself in the inner sanctum of the emergency unit.

She'd timed it well, Izzy thought to herself.

By the time she'd put her bag in her locker, it would be almost time to start, which meant that she could bypass the staffroom, the small talk...

'Izzy!' Beth, an RN she'd worked with over the years, was racing past. 'Cubicle four... Everyone's tied up... She just presented...'

Except Jess *had* been right.

There would be no gentle easing in, Izzy fast realised as Les, the porter, relieved her of her bag. Beth brought her up to speed as best she could in short rapid sentences as they sped across the unit.

'About twenty-three weeks pregnant, though she's vague on dates,' the rapid handover went on. 'She won't make it to Maternity, I've put out a call...'

'Who's seen her?' Izzy asked as she squirted some alcohol rub on her hands.

'You,' came Beth's response

Oh, yes!

She'd forgotten just how unforgiving Emergency could be at times. Just then she saw Ben, wrapping a plastic apron around himself, and Izzy was quite sure he'd take over and usher her off to Section B.

'Have you got this?' Ben said instead, calling over his shoulder as he sped off to Resus.

'Sure!'

'Her name's Nicola,' Beth said as Izzy took one, very quick, deep breath and stepped in.

'Hi, there Nicola. I'm Izzy Bailey, the emergency registrar.' Izzy wasn't sure who looked more petrified, the student nurse who'd been left with the patient while Beth had dashed for a delivery pack or the mother-to-be who brought Izzy up to date with her rapid progress even before Izzy had time to ask more questions—it was Nicola who pulled back the sheet.

'It's coming.'

'Okay.' Izzy pulled on some gloves as Beth opened the delivery pack, Nicola was in no state to be sped across the floor to Resus. 'Let Resus know to expect the baby,' Izzy said. 'Tell them to get a cot ready.' She took a steadying breath. 'Emergency-page the paediatric team.'

'Vivienne!' Beth instructed the student nurse to carry out Izzy's instructions, and Vivienne sped off.

'There's going to be a lot of overhead chimes,' Izzy explained to Nicola, 'but that's just so we can get the staff we need down here quickly for your baby.'

The membrane was intact, Izzy could see it bulging, and she used those few seconds to question her patient a little more, but there were no straightforward answers.

'I only found out last week. I've got a seven-month-old, I'm breastfeeding…'

'Have you had an ultrasound?' Izzy asked.

'She's just come from there,' Beth said for Nicola, but, as was so often the case in Emergency, a neat list of answers rarely arrived with the patient. They would have to be answered later, because this baby was ready to be born.

He slipped into the world a few seconds later, just as

a breathless midwife arrived from Maternity and the overhead speaker chimed its request for the paediatric team to come to Emergency. He was still wrapped in the membrane that should have embraced him for many months more and Izzy parted it, using balloon suction to clear his airway. He was pale and stunned, but stirring into life as Izzy cut the cord. Though outwardly calm, her heart was hammering, because difficult decisions lay ahead for this tiny little man.

'You have a son,' Izzy said, wrapping him up and holding him up briefly for Nicola to see. Though seconds counted in the race for his life, Izzy made one of the many rapid decisions her job entailed and brought the baby up to the mother's head, letting her have a brief glimpse of him. Nicola kissed his little cheek, telling him that she loved him, but those few brief seconds were all there was time for.

Beth had already raced over to Resus, and Izzy left Nicola in the safe hands of the midwife and student nurse as she walked quickly over to Resus holding the infant. A man, dressed in black jeans and a T-shirt, joined her. Walking alongside her, he spoke with a heavy accent.

'What do we know?'

'Mum's dates are hazy,' Izzy said, and though he had no ID on him, there was an air of authority to him that told her this was no nosey relative. 'About twenty-three weeks.'

'Mierda!' Izzy more than understood his curse—she was thinking the same—this tiny baby hovered right on the edge of viability. At this stage of pregnancy every

day *in utero* mattered, but now he was in their hands and they could only give the tiny baby their best care and attention.

'Diego.' Beth looked up from the warming cot she was rapidly preparing. 'That was quick.' The chimes had only just stopped summoning the staff, but he answered in that rich accent, and Izzy realised he was Spanish.

'I was just passing on my way for a late shift.' He had taken the baby from Izzy and was already getting to work, skilfully suctioning the airway as Izzy placed red dots on the baby's tiny chest. 'I heard the call and I figured you could use me.'

They certainly could!

His large hands were rubbing the baby, trying to stimulate it, and Izzy was incredibly grateful he was there. His dark hair was wet so he must have stepped straight out of the shower before coming to work. He had gone completely overboard on the cologne, the musky scent of him way too heavy for a hospital setting. Still, she was very glad he was there. As an emergency doctor, Izzy was used to dealing with crises, but such a premature baby required very specific skills and was terrifying to handle—Diego was clearly used to it and it showed.

'Diego's the neonatal...' Beth paused. 'What *is* your title, Diego?'

'They are still deciding! Sorry...' Dark brown eyes met Izzy's and amidst controlled chaos he squeezed in a smile. 'I should have introduced myself. I'm Nurse Manager on the neonatal unit.'

'I guessed you weren't a passing relative,' Izzy said, but he wasn't listening, his concentration back on the baby. He was breathing, but his chest was working hard, bubbles at his nose and lips, and his nostrils were flaring as he struggled to drag in oxygen.

'We need his history,' Diego said as he proceeded to bag the baby, helping him to breathe. He was skilled and deft and even though the team was just starting to arrive he already had this particular scene under control. 'You're late.' Diego managed dry humour as the anaesthetist rushed in along with the on-call obstetrician and then Izzy's colleague and friend Megan.

Her fragile looks defied her status. Megan was a paediatric registrar and was the jewel in the paediatric team—fighting for her charges' lives, completely devoted to her profession. Her gentle demeanour defied her steely determination when a life hung in the balance.

Megan would, Izzy knew, give the baby every benefit of every doubt.

'Ring NICU.' This was Diego, giving orders, even though it wasn't his domain. They urgently needed more equipment. Even the tiniest ET tube was proving too big for this babe and feeling just a touch superfluous as Megan and Diego worked on, it was Izzy who made the call to the neonatal intensive care unit, holding the phone to Diego's ear as he rapidly delivered his orders.

Though Megan's long brown hair was tied back, the run from the children's ward had caused a lock to come loose and she gave a soft curse as she tried to concentrate on getting an umbilical line into the baby.

'Here,' Izzy said, and sorted out her friend's hair.

'*About* twenty-three weeks, Megan.' Diego said it as

a warning as the baby's heart rate dipped ominously low, but his warning was vital.

'We don't know anything for sure!' Megan words were almost chanted as she shot a warning at Diego. 'I'll do a proper maturation assessment once he's more stable. Izzy, can you start compressions while I get this line in?'

Diego was pulling up the minuscule drug dosages; the anaesthetist taking over in helping the tiny baby to breathe. The baby was so small Izzy compressed the chest rapidly with two fingers, hearing the rapid rhythm on the monitor.

'Nice work.' Megan was always encouraging. The umbilical line in, she took the drugs from Diego and shot them into the little body as Izzy carried on with compressions for another full minute.

'Let's see what we've got.' Megan put a hand up to halt Izzy and the babe's heart rate was up now close to a hundred. There were more staff arriving and a large incubator had arrived from the neonatal unit along with more specialised equipment, but until the baby was more stable it wouldn't be moved up to the first-floor NICU. 'We're going to be here for a while.' Megan gave Izzy a grim smile. 'Sorry to take up all your space.'

'Go right ahead,' Izzy said.

'How are things?' an unfamiliar face came in. 'Ben asked me check in—I'm Josh, A and E consultant.' She'd heard there was a new consultant, that he was Irish and women everywhere were swooning, but no one was swooning here! Izzy couldn't really explain it, but suddenly the mood in the room changed. Izzy wondered if perhaps if Josh's popularity had plummeted, because there was certainly a chill in the air.

'It's all under control.' It was Izzy who broke the strange silence. 'Though the babe might be here for a while.'

'How many weeks?' Josh's voice was gruff, his navy eyes narrowing as he looked down at the tiny infant.

'We're not sure yet,' Megan responded. 'Mum was in Ultrasound when she went into labour.'

'We need to find out.' Josh's was the voice of reason. Before there were any more heroics, some vital facts needed to be established. 'Do you want me to speak with Mum?'

'I'll be the one who speaks with the mother.' Megan's voice was pure ice. 'But right now I'm a bit tied up.'

'There's a full resuscitation taking place in my department on a baby that may not be viable—we need to find out what the mother wants.'

Megan looked up and Izzy was shocked at the blaze of challenge in them. 'It's not like it was eight years ago. We don't wrap them in a blanket now and say we can't do anything for them.'

'I'll tell you what!' A thick Spanish accent waded into the tense debate and abruptly resolved it. 'While you two sort out your own agenda, why don't you...' he looked over at Izzy '...go and speak with the mother? You have already met her, after all. See if you can clarify the dates a bit better—let her know just how ill the baby is and find out if someone can pull up her ultrasound images.'

'Sure!'

She was more than grateful for Diego's presence, and not just for the baby—Izzy hadn't known what was happening in there. She'd never seen Megan like that! Her response had been a blatant snub to Josh's offer to speak with the mother, but Izzy didn't have time to dwell on it—instead she had a most difficult conversation in front of her.

'I don't know...' Nicola sobbed as Izzy gently questioned her. 'My periods are so irregular and it's my fourth baby, I was breast feeding...'

'The doctors will go through your scans and assess your baby and try to get the closest date we can,' Izzy said gently, 'but I have to tell you that things aren't looking very good for your son.' Izzy suddenly felt guilty talking about this to the mother when she was pregnant herself, and was incredibly grateful when Diego came into the cubicle. He gave her a thin smile and, because he would be more than used to this type of conversation, Izzy allowed him to take over.

'Another one of my staff is in with your baby,' he said, having introduced himself to the mother, and did what Megan had insisted Josh didn't. Izzy felt the sting of tears in her eyes as very skilfully, very gently Diego talked Nicola through all that had happened, all that was now taking place and all that could lie ahead if her baby were to survive.

'Right now,' Diego said, 'we are doing everything we can to save your baby, but he is in a very fragile state. Nicola. Do you understand what I said to you about the risks, about the health problems your baby might face if he does survive?'

'Do everything you can.'

'We will,' Diego said. 'Megan, the paediatrician, will come in and speak at more length with you, but right now she needs to be in with your son.' He was very kind, but also very firm. 'We're going to be moving him up to the NICU shortly, but why don't I get you a wheelchair and we can take you in to see him before we head off?'

To Izzy it was too soon, Resus was still a hive of activity, but she also knew that Diego was right, that maybe Nicola needed to see for herself the lengths to which they were going to save the baby and also that, realistically, this might be Nicola's only chance to see her son alive.

She didn't get to hold him, but Diego did ask for a camera and took some pictures of Nicola next to her son, and some close-up shots of the baby. And then it was time for him to be moved.

'Nice work,' he said to Izzy as his team moved off with its precious cargo, Diego choosing to stay behind. 'Thank you for everything, and sorry to leave so much mess. I'm going to have a quick run-through of your equipment, if that's okay. There are a few things you ought to order.'

'That would be great,' Izzy said. 'And thank you. You've been marvellous!'

'Marvellous!' He repeated the word as if were the first time he'd heard it and grinned, his teeth were so white, so perfect. If the rest of him hadn't been so divine, she'd have sworn they were capped. 'You were *marvellous* too!' Then his eyes narrowed in closer assessment.

'You're new?' Diego checked, because even though he was rarely in Emergency he was quite sure that he'd have noticed her around the hospital.

'No. I've worked here for ages. I've been on...' She didn't really know what to say so she settled for a very simple version. 'Extended leave.' She gave him a wide smile. 'You're the one who's new.'

'How do you know that?' He raised the most perfectly shaped eyebrow, and if eyes could smile, his were. 'I might have been here for years. Perhaps I did my training here...' He was teasing her, with a question she was less prepared to deal with than a premature birth. 'Why do you think I'm new?'

Because I'd have noticed you.

That was the answer and they both knew it.

Now there was no baby, now there was no emergency to deal with, now it was just the two of them, Izzy, for the first time in, well, the longest time, looked at a man.

Not saw.

Looked.

And as she did so, the strangest thing happened—the four months of endless chatter in her head was silenced. For a delicious moment the fear abated and all she was was a woman.

A woman whose eyes lingered for a fraction too long on a beautiful man.

His hair had dried now and she noticed it was long enough to be sexy and short enough to scrape in as smart. He was a smudge unshaven, but Izzy guessed that even if he met a razor each morning, that shadow would be back in time for lunch. Even in jeans and a T-shirt, even without the olive skin and deep accent, there was a dash of the European about him—his black jeans just a touch tighter, his T-shirt from no high street store that Izzy frequented. He was professional and he was well groomed, but there was a breath of danger about him, a dizzy, musky air that brought Izzy back to a woman she had once known.

'Well,' he said when the silence had gone on too long, 'it's nice to stand here *chatting*, but I have to get back.'

'Of course.'

'A porter took my bag. Do you know where I can find him?'

'Your bag?' Izzy blinked, because it was the sort of thing she would say, but rather than work that one out, she went and called the porter over the Tannoy.

'Come up and see him later,' Diego suggested.

'I will,' Izzy said, consoling herself that he would have extended that invitation to any doctor, that the invitation wasn't actually for her, that it had nothing to do with him.

Except Diego corrected her racing thoughts.

'I'm on till ten.'

What on earth was that?

She'd never been on a horse, yet she felt as if she'd just been galloping at breakneck speed along the beach. Izzy headed for the staffroom, in need of a cool drink of water before she tackled the next patient, wanting to get her scrambled brain into some sort of order after the adrenaline rush of earlier.

A premature delivery would do that to anyone, Izzy told herself as she grabbed a cup. Except, as a large lazy bubble in the water cooler rose and popped to the surface, she felt as if she were seeing her insides spluttering into life after the longest sleep.

She couldn't have been flirting.

She was in no position to be flirting.

Except, Izzy knew, she had been.

They had been.

The lone figure in the staffroom caught her by surprise and Izzy had begun to back out when she saw who it was. Josh was sitting there, head in hands, his face grey, and Izzy was quite sure she was intruding.

'Don't go on my account,' Josh said. 'I was just heading back. How is she?' he asked.

'Upset,' Izzy admitted. 'I think she was only just getting used to the idea of being pregnant, but...' Her voice trailed off, Josh nodded and stood up and walked out, but before that, even as she spoke, realisation dawned.

Josh hadn't been enquiring how the mother was.

Instead he'd been asking about Megan.

CHAPTER THREE

'ARE you sure you don't want me to stay and help clear the board?' Izzy checked as the clock edged towards ten.

'Go home and get some well-earned rest,' Ben said. 'You haven't had the easiest start back.'

'And I thought you'd break me in gently.'

'Not my style,' Ben said. 'You did great, Izzy. Mind you, you look like you've been dragged through a hedge!'

The power dressing had lasted till about three p.m. when she had changed into more familiar scrubs, her mascara was smudged beneath her eyes and her mouth devoid of lipstick.

It had been Chest Pain Central for the rest of the shift and apart from two minutes on the loo, Izzy had not sat down.

'One day,' Izzy said, 'I'm going to manage to stay in my own clothes for an entire shift. I am!' she insisted as Josh joined them. She'd had a good shift. Josh had been lovely—as sharp as a tack, he had been a pleasure to work with, his strong Irish brogue already familiar to Izzy.

'It will never happen!' Josh said. 'I thought the same—that maybe when I made consultant... I had some nice suits made, didn't I, Ben?'

They had been friends for years, Izzy had found out, had both worked together in London, and as Izzy grinned and wished them both goodnight she was glad now about her decision to return to work.

It *was* good to be back.

The patients didn't care about the doctor's personal life, didn't know the old Izzy, they just accepted her. Any doubts she might have had about the wisdom of coming back at such a fragile time emotionally had soon faded as she had immersed herself in the busy hub of Emergency, stretching her brain instead of being stuck in that awful loop of wandering around her home, thinking.

It was only now, as she stepped out of her professional role, that the smile faded.

She didn't want to go home.

She stared out past the ambulance bay to the staff car park and she felt a bubble of panic. She could call Security to escort her, of course. Given what had happened, who would blame her for not wanting to walk though the car park alone.

It wasn't even dark. It was one of those lovely summer nights in St Piran when the sky never became fully black.

It wasn't just the car park she was afraid of, though,

she decided as she turned and headed up the corridor to the stairwell.

She just wasn't ready to go home.

Her fingers hovered over the NICU intercom, wondering what exactly she was doing. Usually she wouldn't have thought twice about this. The old Izzy had often popped up to the wards to check on cases she had seen in Emergency, but her pregnant status made it seem more personal somehow and it wasn't just the baby she had delivered that had drawn her there tonight. Still, despite more than a passing thought about him now as she neared his territory, it wasn't just Diego pulling her there either—it was after ten, the late staff would long since have gone.

There was a very private answer she was seeking tonight.

It *was* more personal because she was pregnant, Izzy admitted to herself. She wasn't just here to see how the baby was doing, rather to see her reaction to it, to see if the little scrap she had delivered that morning might somehow evoke in her some feeling for the babe she was carrying.

She was being ridiculous, Izzy told herself, as if a trip to the NICU would put her mind at ease.

Turning on her heel, Izzy decided against visiting.

She'd ring the NICU tomorrow and find out how he was doing.

'Hey!' Having made up her mind and turned go, Izzy jumped slightly as the doors opened and she was greeted by the sound of Diego's voice.

Even before she turned and saw him, even though it

was just one syllable he'd uttered, she knew that it was him and she felt her cheeks colour up, wondering what reason she could give as to why she was there.

'You're here to see your delivery?' He wasn't really looking at her; instead he was turning on his phone and checking the messages that pinged in.

'If that's okay…' She was incredibly nervous around him, flustered even, her words coming out too fast as she offered too much of an explanation. 'I often chase up interesting cases. I know it's a bit late, so I decided to ring tomorrow…'

'Day and night are much the same in there,' he said. 'It won't be a problem.'

'I'll just ring tomorrow. I'm sure they're busy'

She'd changed her mind before she'd seen him, yet Diego wouldn't hear it.

'One moment,' he said. 'I'll take you in. Let me just answer this.'

She didn't want him to take her in.

She glanced at the ID badge he now had around his neck.

Diego Ramirez was so not what she needed now.

Still, he was too engrossed in his phone to read her body language, Izzy thought. His *bag* was a large brown leather satchel, which he wore over his shoulder, and on *anyone* else it would have looked, well, stupid, but it just set him aside from the others.

God, what was it about him?

Diego didn't need to look at Izzy to read her. He could *feel* her tense energy, knew she was nervous, and he knew enough to know that a pregnant woman who had delivered a prem baby would, perhaps, have a few questions or need a little reassurance.

Any of his staff could provide that, Diego said to himself as he checked his message from Sally.

The term 'girlfriend' for Sally, would be stretching it, but she *was* gorgeous and she was sitting outside his flat in a car right this minute, texting to see when he'd be home.

He loved women.

He loved curves on women.

He loved confident women

He loved lots of uninhibited, straightforward sex—and it was right there waiting at his door.

Busy at work—txt u tomoz x

Not regretfully enough he hit 'send', but he did wonder what on earth he was doing. Why, instead of heading for home, he was swiping his ID card to gain entry into the area and walking this slinky-malinky long-legs, who was as jumpy as a cat, through his unit?

'Wash your hands,' Diego prompted, following his own instructions and soaping up his hands and rather large forearms for an inordinate amount of time. 'It is a strict rule here,' he explained, 'and one I enforce, no matter the urgency. And,' he chided as Izzy turned off the handle with her elbow, 'I also ask that staff take an extra moment more than is deemed necessary.'

Oh.

Chastised and not liking it a bit, Izzy turned the tap on again and recommenced the rather long ritual.

'I do know how to wash my hands.'

He didn't answer.

'I don't have to be told.'

He turned and looked at her rigid profile.

'Yes, Doctor, you do.' He turned off the tap and pulled out a wad of paper towels. 'Doctors are the worst culprits.'

She rolled her eyes and he just laughed.

'By the way,' Diego said. 'I'm not.'

It was Izzy who didn't answer now, just pursed her lips a touch as she dried her own hands, refusing to give him the satisfaction of asking what the hell he was talking about. Instead she followed him through NICU, past the endless incubators, most with their own staff member working quietly on the occupant.

It was incredibly noisy—Izzy remembered that from her paediatric rotation, but she'd been such a confident young thing then, curious more than nervous. Now it seemed that every bleep, every noise made her jump.

'Here he is. Toby is his name.' Diego looked down into the incubator then spoke with the nurse who was looking after the infant Izzy had, just that afternoon, delivered. Yet when he glanced over at the rather brittle doctor he found himself momentarily distracted, watching Izzy frown down at the tiny infant, then watching as her huge eyes darted around the large ward, then back to the baby.

'He's doing well,' Diego explained, 'though it is minute by minute at the moment—he's extremely premature, but Megan has done a thorough maturation assessment and thinks he's more like twenty-four weeks.'

'That's good news,' Izzy said, only Diego didn't look particularly convinced. 'Well, it's good that she delivered in hospital,' Izzy said, 'even if she was in the wrong department.' She stared at the baby and as she felt her own kicking she willed herself, begged herself to feel something, this surge of connection to her own babe that she knew she should feel.

'Do you get attached?' Izzy asked, and Diego shook his head.

'Too dangerous here. It's the parents who get to me if anything.'

She'd seen enough. The baby was tiny and fragile and she hoped and prayed he would be okay, but the bells weren't ringing for her, the clouds weren't parting. There was no sudden flood of emotion, other than she suddenly felt like crying, but only because of her lack of feeling for her own baby she carried. 'Well, thank you very much.' She gave a tight smile. 'As I said, I just thought I'd pop in on my way home.'

'I'll walk with you,' Diego offered.

'There no need.' Izzy said, but he ignored her and fell into step beside her. She really wished he wouldn't, she just wanted out of the stifling place, away from the machines and equipment, away from babies, away from the endless guilt...

'How far along are you?'

'Sorry?'

'How many weeks pregnant?'

She was momentarily sideswiped by his boldness and also glad for the normality of his question. It was the question everyone *hadn't* asked today—the bump that everyone, bar Jess, seemed to studiously avoid mentioning.

'Twenty-eight weeks,' Izzy said. 'Well, almost,' she continued, but she had lost her audience. Diego had stopped walking and she turned her head to where he stood.

'Here.'

Izzy frowned.

'Over here.' Diego beckoned her over and after a slight hesitation she followed him, coming to a stop at an incubator where a tiny baby lay. Tiny, but comparatively much larger than the little boy she had delivered that afternoon. 'This little one is almost twenty-nine weeks, aren't you, *bebé*?' Diego crooned, then pumped some alcohol rub into his hands. 'You're awake...'

'I thought you said you didn't get attached!' Izzy grinned and so too did the nurse looking after the little girl.

'If that's Diego detached,' joked the nurse, as Diego stroked her little cheek and chatted on in Spanish, 'then we're all dying to see him in love.'

'She's *exceptionally* cute,' Diego said. 'She was a twenty-four-weeker too, though girls are tougher than boys. She's a real fighter...' His voice seemed to fade out then, though Izzy was sort of aware that he was still talking, except she didn't really have room in her head to process anything else other than the baby she was looking at.

This was what was inside her now.

This was what had bought her up to the NICU tonight—a need for some sort of connection to the baby growing inside her. And Diego had led her to it.

Her little eyes were open, her hands stretching, her face scrunching up, her legs kicking, and Izzy watched, transfixed, as the nurse fed her, holding up a syringe of milk and letting gravity work as the syringe emptied through the tube into the infant's stomach as Diego gave her a teat to suck on so she would equate the full feeling with suckling.

'She's perfect,' Izzy said.

'She's doing well,' Diego said. 'We're all really pleased with her.' He glanced at Izzy. 'I imagine it's hard to take in.'

'Very,' Izzy admitted.

'Come on,' he said, when she had stood and looked for a moment or two longer. 'You should be home and resting after they day you've had.' They walked together more easily now, Izzy stopping at the vending machine and trying to choose between chocolate and chocolate.

'You'll spoil your dinner.'

'This is dinner!' Izzy said, and then grimaced, remembering who she was talking to. 'I mean, I'll have something sensible when I get home...'

He just laughed.

'Don't beat yourself up over a bar of chocolate!' Diego said. 'You need lots of calories now, to fatten that baby up.' He could see the effort it took for her just to sustain that smile. 'And you need to relax; they pick up on things.'

'I do relax.'

'Good.'

He fished in his satchel and pulled out a brown bag. 'Here, Brianna forgot to take them.'

'What are they?' For a moment she thought they were sweets. 'Tomatoes?'

'Cherry tomatoes.'

'Miniature cherry tomatoes,' Izzy said peering into the bag. 'Mini-miniature cherry tomatoes.'

'Keep them in the bag and the green ones will redden. I grow them,' Diego said, then corrected himself. 'I grew them.' He frowned. 'Grow or grew? Sometimes I choose the wrong word.'

They were outside now, heading for the car park..

Izzy thought for a moment and it was so nice to think about something so mundane. 'Grow *or* grew. You grow them and you grew these.'

'Thank you, teacher!'

He was rewarded by her first genuine smile and she looked at him again. 'So what's this about your job title?' Izzy remembered a conversation from Resus.

'The powers that be are revising our titles and job descriptions. Two meetings, eight memos and guess what they came up with?' He nudged her as they walked. 'Guess.'

'I can't.'

'Modern Matron!' She could hear someone laughing and realised with a jolt it was her. Not a false laugh but a real laugh, and then he made her laugh some more. 'I said, "Not without a dress!" And I promise I will wear one; if that is the title they give me. Can you imagine when my family rings me at work.' He glanced at her.

'Surgeons, all of them. I'm the *oveja negra*, the black sheep.'

'I like black sheep,' Izzy said, and then wished she hadn't, except it had honestly just slipped out.

They were at her car now and instead of saying goodnight, Izzy lingered. He was sexy and gorgeous but he was also wise and kind and, despite herself, somehow she trusted him, trusted him with more than she had trusted anyone in a very long time.

'You said that babies can pick up on things…' Izzy swallowed. 'Do you believe that?'

'It's proven,' Diego said.

'So if you're stressed or not happy…'

'They know.'

'And if you're not sure…' She wanted him to jump in, but he didn't, he just continued to lean on her car. She should just get in it. Surely she should just drive off rather than admit what she didn't dare to. 'I mean, do you think they could know if you don't…?' She couldn't say it, but Diego did.

'If you don't want them?'

'Shh!' Izzy scolded, appalled at his choice of words.

'Why?' There was a lazy smile on his face that was absolutely out of place with the seriousness of her admission. 'It can't understand your words—they're not *that* clever.'

'Even so!' She was annoyed now, but he just carried on smiling. 'You don't say things like that.'

'Not to an over-protective mum!'

Oh!

She'd never thought of it like that, never thought that her refusal to voice her thoughts, her refusal to even let herself properly *think* them might, in fact, show that she did have feelings for the life inside.

It was her darkest fear.

Of the many things that kept her brain racing through sleepless nights, this was the one that she dreaded exploring most—that her feelings for her baby's father might somehow translate to her baby.

That love might not grow.

'You're not the only woman to be unsure she's ready,' Diego said. 'And lots of mothers-to-be are stressed and unhappy, but I'm sure you're not stressed and unhappy *all* the time.' His smile faded when she didn't agree and they stood for a quiet moment.

'What if I am?'

He was silent for a while, unsure why a woman so beautiful, so vibrant, so competent would be so unhappy, but it wasn't his business and for a dangerous moment Diego wished it was. So instead he smiled. 'You can fake it.'

'Fake it?'

'Fake it!' Diego nodded, that gorgeous smile in full flood now. 'As I said, they're not *that* clever. Twice a day, fake happiness, say all the things you think you should be saying, dance around the house, go for a walk on the beach, swim. I do each morning, whether I feel like it or not.'

He so didn't get it, but, then, how could he?

'Thanks for the suggestions.' She gave him her best bright smile and pulled out her keys.

'Goodnight, then.'

'Where are you parked?'

'I'm not. I live over there.' He pointed in the direction of the beach. 'I walk to work.'

'You didn't have to escort me.'

'I enjoyed it,' he said. 'Anyway, you shouldn't be walking through car parks on your own at night.'

He really didn't get it, Izzy realised.

He was possibly the only person in the hospital who didn't know her past, or he'd never have said what he just had.

She turned on the engine and as she slid into reverse he knocked on her car window and, irritated now, she wound it down.

'Sing in the shower!' He said. 'Twice a day.'

'Sure' Izzy rolled her eyes. Like *that* was going to help.

'And by the way ,' he said as she was about to close her window, 'I'm not!'

Izzy pulled on her handbrake and let the engine idle and she looked at those lips and those eyes and that smile and she realised exactly why she was annoyed— was she flirting?

Did twenty-eight weeks pregnant, struggling mentally to just survive, recently widowed women ever even begin to think about flirting?

No.

Because had she thought about it she would never have wound down that window some more.

'Not what?' Izzy asked the question she had refused to ask earlier, her cheeks just a little pink.

'I'm not a frustrated doctor,' Diego said, 'as many of your peers seem to think every male nurse is.'

'Glad to hear it,' Izzy said, and took off the hand-brake, the car moving slowly beside him.

'And I'm not the other cliché either!' he called, and her cheeks were on fire, yet for the first time in the longest time she was grinning. Not forcing a smile, no, she was, from ear to ear, grinning.

No, there was absolutely no chance that Diego Ramirez was gay!

'I'd already worked that out!' Izzy called as she pushed up her window. 'Night, Diego!'

'It went well, Mum!' Izzy buttered some toast as she spoke to her mother and added some ginger marmalade. 'Though it was strange being back *after*...' Izzy stopped, because her mother didn't like talking about *before*, so instead she chatted some more, told her mum about Toby, but her mum didn't take the lead and made no mention of Izzy's pregnancy.

'So you had a good day?' her mother checked as Izzy idly opened the brown paper bag and took out a handful of tiny tomatoes. They tasted fantastic, little squirts of summer popping on her tongue, helping Izzy to inject some enthusiasm into her voice.

'Marvellous,' Izzy said, smiling at the choice of word and remembering Diego's smile.

It was actually a relief to hang up.

She was so damn tired of putting others at ease.

So *exhausted* wearing the many different Izzy masks...

Doctor Izzy.

To add to Daughter Izzy.

Domestic Abuse Victim Izzy.

Grieving Izzy.

Mother-to-be Izzy.

Coping Izzy.

She juggled each ball, accepted another as it was tossed in, and sometimes, *sometimes* she'd like to drop the lot, except she knew she wouldn't.

Couldn't.

She could remember her mother's horror when she had for a moment dropped the coping pretence and chopped off her hair. Izzy could still see the pain in her mother's eyes and simply wouldn't put her through it any more.

Oh, but she wanted to, Izzy thought, running her bath and undressing, catching sight of herself in the mirror, her blonde hair way-too-short, her figure too thin for such a pregnant woman.

How she'd love to ring her mum back—ask her to come over, to *take* over.

Except she knew she couldn't.

Wouldn't.

Since that night, there had been a huge wedge between them and Izzy truly didn't know how to fix it. She just hoped that one day it would be fixed, that maybe when the baby came things would improve. Except her mother could hardly bring herself to talk about the impending arrival.

Damn Henry Bailey!

Whoosh!

The anger that Jess had told her was completely normal, was a 'good sign', in fact, came rushing in then and, yes, she should do as Jess said perhaps, and write pages and pages in her journal, or shout, or cry, or read the passage in her self-help book on anger.

Except she was too tired for Henry tonight.

Too fed up to deal with her so-called healthy anger.

Too bone weary to shout or cry.

She wanted a night off!

So she lit six candles instead, the relaxing ones apparently, and lay there and waited for them to work, except they didn't.

She *had* to relax.

It was important for the baby!

Oh, and it would be so easy to cry now, but instead she sat up and pulled the plug out, and then she had another idea, or rather she decided to try out Diego's idea.

She'd fake it.

Cramming the plug back in the hole, she topped up with hot water and feeling stupid, feeling beyond stupid, she lay back as the hot water poured over her toes and she sang the happiest song she could think of.

A stupid happy song.

And then another.

Then she sang a love song, at the top of her voice at midnight, in her smart townhouse.

And she was used to the neighbours banging on the walls during one of her and Henry's fights, so it didn't really faze her when they did just that. Instead she sang louder.

Izzy just lay there in the bath, faking being happy, till her baby was kicking and she was grinning—and even if, for now, she had to fake it, thanks to a male nurse who wasn't a frustrated doctor and certainly wasn't the other cliché, by the time her fingers and toes were all shrivelled up, Izzy wasn't actually sure if she was faking it.

For a second there, if she didn't analyse it too much, if she just said it as it was…

Well, she could have almost passed as happy!

CHAPTER FOUR

DIEGO was not in the best of moods.

Not that anyone would really know.

Though laid back in character, he was always firm in the running of his unit. His babies came first and though friendly and open in communication, he kept a slight distance from his staff that was almost indefinable.

Oh, he chatted. They knew he loved to swim in the Cornish sea, that he came from an affluent long line of doctors in Madrid, they even knew that he was somewhat estranged from his family due to his career choice, for Diego would roll his eyes if any of them rang him at work. His staff knew too about his rather pacy love life—the dark-eyed, good-looking Spaniard was never short of a date but, much to many a St Piran's female staff member's disgust, he never dated anyone from work.

No, the stunning women who occasionally dropped in, waiting for him to finish his shift, or called him on the phone, had nothing to do with hospitals—not public ones anyway. Their hospital stays tended to be in private clinics for little *procedures* to enhance their already polished looks.

There was just this certain aloofness to Diego—an independent thinker, he never engaged in gossip or mixed his private life with his work.

So no one knew that, despite his zealous attention to detail with his precious charges that day, there was a part of Diego that was unusually distracted.

Cross with himself even.

Okay, his relations with women veered more towards sexual than emotional, and if his moral code appeared loose to some, it actually came with strict guidelines—it was always exclusive. And, a man of honour, he knew it was wrong to suddenly be taking his lunches in the canteen instead of on the ward and looking out for that fragile beauty who was clearly taken.

Wrong, so very wrong to have been thinking of her late, *very late*, into the night.

But why *was* she so stressed and unhappy?

If she were his partner, he'd make damn sure...

Diego blew out a breath, blocked that line of thought and carried on typing up the complicated handover sheet, filling in the updates on his charges, now that Rita the ward clerk had updated the admissions and discharges and changes of cots. It was Monday and there was always a lot to be updated. It was a job he loathed, but he did it quicker and more accurately than anyone else and it was a good way of keeping current with all the patients, even if he couldn't be hands on with them all. So Diego spent a long time on the sheet—speaking with each staff member in turn, checking up on each baby in his care. The NICU handover sheet was a lesson in excellence.

'I'm still trying to chase up some details for Baby Geller,' Rita informed him as Diego typed in the three-days-old latest treatment regime. 'Maternity hasn't sent over forms.'

'He came via Emergency.' Diego didn't look up. 'After you left on Friday.'

'That's right—the emergency obstetric page that went out.' Rita went through his paperwork. 'Do you know the delivering doctor? I need to go to Maternity and get some forms then I can send it all down and he can fill it in.'

'She.' Diego tried to keep his deep voice nonchalant. 'Izzy Bailey, and I think I've got some of the forms in my office. I can take them down.'

'Is she back?' Rita sounded shocked. 'After all that's happened you'd think she'd have stayed off till after the baby. Mind you, the insurance aren't paying up, I've heard. They're dragging their feet, saying it might be suicide—as if! No doubt the poor thing *has* to work.'

Diego hated gossip and Rita was an expert in it. Nearing retirement, she had been there for ever and made everyone's business her own. Rita's latest favourite topic was Megan the paediatrician, who she watched like a hawk, or Brianna Flannigan, the most private of nurses, but today Rita clearly had another interest. Normally Diego would have carried on working or told her to be quiet, but curiosity had the better of him and, not proud of himself, Diego prolonged the unsavoury conversation.

'Suicide?' Diego turned around. 'Are you talking about Izzy's husband?'

'Henry Bailey!' Rita nodded. 'It wasn't suicide, of course; he just drove off in a blind rage. She'd left him, but he turned up at work, waited for her in the car park...' She flushed a little, perhaps aware that she was being terribly indiscreet and that Diego was normally the one to halt her. 'I'm not speaking out of turn; it was all over the newspapers and all over the CCTV, though of course it would have been before you arrived in St Piran's.'

No, it wasn't his proudest morning, because once the handover sheet was complete, Diego headed for his office and closed the door. Feeling as if he was prying but wanting to know all the same, it didn't take long to find out everything Rita had told him and more. Oh, he would never abuse his position and look up personal information, but it was there for everyone, splashed all over the internet, and as he read it he felt his stomach churn in unease for all she had been through.

Pregnant, trying to leave an abusive marriage, real estate agent Henry Bailey had beaten his wife in the darkened hospital car park. Rita was right, the whole, shocking incident had been captured on CCTV and images of footage and the details were spelt out in the press.

He felt sick.

Reading it, he felt physically sick and also strangely proud.

Her first day back.

Mierda! He cursed himself as he remembered his

throw-away comment about the car park. He replayed the conversation they had had over and over and wished he could start with her again.

His door knocked and he quickly clicked away from the page he was viewing, before calling whoever it was to come in, but he felt a rare blush on his cheeks as the woman herself stood before him. Diego actually felt as if he'd been caught snooping as Izzy let herself in, a wide smile on her face, and he wondered how on earth she managed it.

She had leggings on again and a bright red dress with bright red lipstick and, Diego noticed, bright red cheeks as he just continued to stare up at her.

'You need me to sign off on the delivery?' It was Izzy who broke the silence; Diego was momentarily lost for words. 'Your ward clerk just rang...'

'We would have sent them down to you.'

'Oh!' Izzy blushed a shade darker as she lied just a little. 'I thought it sounded urgent.'

'I should have some forms...' He was unusually flustered as he rummaged through his desk. 'Or I'll ring Maternity. Here...' Diego found them and was pathetically grateful when the door knocked and one of his team stood there. with a screaming baby with a familiar request.

'Would you mind?'

'Not at all.' He washed his hands, *thoroughly*, then took the screaming baby and plonked it face down on his forearm, its little head at his elbow, and he rocked it easily as he spoke.

'Genevieve!' he introduced. 'Goes home this week, please God! I do not envy her parents.'

Well, Genevieve looked as if she'd happily stay with Diego for ever! The tears had stopped and she was already almost asleep as he bounced away.

'If you want to get started on the forms I'll just go and get the details you'll need.' He paused at the door. 'I was just about to get a drink…'

'Not for me, thanks,' Izzy said, and then changed her mind. 'Actually, water would be great.'

'Would you mind…?' It was his turn to say it and he gestured to the baby. Izzy went to put out her hands and then laughed.

'Joking!' she said, then went over to his sink and *thoroughly* washed hers. 'Am I clean enough for you?'

Oh, God, there was an answer there!

And they just both stood there, looking a bit stunned.

Izzy flaming red, Diego biting down on his tongue rather than tell her he'd prefer her dirty.

And thank God for Miss Genevieve or he might just have kissed her face off!

Diego got them both water.

Well, he couldn't do much with two polystyrene cups and tap water but he did go to the ice dispenser and then had a little chat with himself in his head as he walked back to his office.

What the hell was wrong with him?

He hardly knew her, she was pregnant, and she obviously had *major* issues.

Why was he acting like a twelve-year-old walking

past the underwear department in a department store? Nervous, jumpy, embarrassed, hell, he couldn't actually fancy her, and even if he did, normally that didn't pose a problem—he fancied loads of women.

This, though, felt different.

Maybe he felt sorry for her? Diego wondered as he balanced a file under his arm and two cups in one big hand and opened his office door.

But, no, he'd been thinking about her long before Rita had told him what had happened.

Then she looked up from the form she was filling in and smiled, and Diego was tempted to turn round and walk out.

He more than fancied her.

Not liked, not felt sorry for, no. As he washed his hands and took Genevieve from her and sat down behind his desk it wasn't sympathy that was causing this rather awkward reaction.

Diego was used to women.

Beautiful women.

Ordinary women.

Postnatal women.

Pregnant women were regular visitors to his unit— often he walked a mum-to-be around his unit, telling her what to expect once her baby was born.

He was more than used to women, yet not one, not one single one, had ever had this effect on him.

'How is Toby doing?' Izzy looked up from the forms and Diego made a wobbly gesture with one hand.

'Can I have a peek?' Izzy signed off her name and then reached for her water. 'I'm done.'

'Sure,' Diego said. 'I'll put this one down and take you over—we've moved him.'

Genevieve was sleeping now, and Izzy walked with him to the nursery. It was a far more relaxed atmosphere there.

There were about eight babies, all in clear cribs and dressed in their own clothes, the parents more relaxed and, Izzy noticed, everyone had a smile when Diego walked in and put Genevieve back in her cot.

He was certainly popular, Izzy thought as they head back out to the busy main floor of NICU.

'You need to—'

'Wash my hands,' Izzy interrupted, 'I know.'

'Actually...' Diego gave a small wince. 'Your perfume is very strong. Perhaps you could...'

'I'm not wearing perfume,' Izzy said as she soaped up her hands, 'and you're hardly one to talk, I can smell your cologne from here!'

'I don't wear cologne for work.'

'Oh.' Izzy glanced over. 'Then what...?' She didn't finish, she just turned back to the taps and concentrated really hard on rinsing off the soap.

She could smell him.

If she breathed in now she could taste him—she'd even commented to Megan on his cologne, but Megan had said... Izzy swallowed as she recalled the flip conversation. Megan hadn't even noticed it...

She could smell him and Diego could smell her and they'd just told each other so.

There was no witty comeback from that.

It was the *most* awkward five minutes of her life.

Okay, not *the most* awkward—the last few months had brought many of them. Rather it was the most pleasantly cringe-making, confusingly awkward five minutes of her life.

She peered at Baby Geller and asked after his mother, Nicola. She tried to remember that breathing was a normal bodily function as the nurse who was looking after the babe asked Diego to hold him for a moment while she changed the bedding. The sight of the tiny baby nestled in his strong arms, resting against his broad chest, was just such a contrast between tenderness and masculinity that it had Izzy almost dizzy with the blizzard of emotions it evoked.

'I'd better get back.' Her mouth felt as if was made of rubber—even a simple sentence was difficult.

She managed a smile and then she turned and walked briskly out of the department. Only once she was safely out did she lean against the wall and close her eyes, breathing as if she'd run up the emergency exit steps. Shocked almost because never in her wildest dreams had she considered this, even ventured the possibility that she might be attracted to someone.

She was so raw, so scared, so just dealing with functioning, let alone coping, that men weren't even on a distant horizon yet.

And yet...

She'd never been so strongly attracted to someone.

Never.

Even in the early days with Henry, before he'd shown his true colours, she hadn't felt like this. Oh, she had loved him, had been so deeply in love she'd been sure of it—only it had felt nothing like this attraction.

An attraction that was animal almost.

She *could* smell the delicious fragrance of him.

Right now, on her skin in her hair, she leant against the wall and dragged in the air, and still his fragrance lingered in her nostrils.

'Izzy!' Her eyes opened to the concerned voice of Jess. 'Are you okay?'

'I'm fine!' She smiled. 'I was just in NICU, and it's so hot in there...' God, she felt like she'd been caught smoking by the headmistress, as if Jess could see the little plumes of smoke coming from behind her back. She tried to carry on as if her world hadn't just upended itself. Jess would hardly be thrilled to hear what was going through her patient's mind now.

It was impossible that it was even going through her mind now.

There wasn't room in her life, in her heart, in her head for even one single extra emotion, let alone six feet two of made-in-Spain testosterone.

'How are you finding it?' Jess asked as they walked in step back to the emergency department, and then Jess gave a kind smile, 'I'm just making conversation...'

'I know.' Izzy grinned and forced herself back to a safer conversation than the one she was having with herself. 'Actually, it's been really nice. It's good having something else to think about.'

Only she wasn't just talking about work.

CHAPTER FIVE

'THE nurses are all tied up and I've got to dash over to the children's ward,' Megan said into the phone. 'I'll ask Izzy.'

'Ask Izzy what?'

She'd been back a full week now.

It was late.

She was tired.

And the patient she was dealing with wasn't exactly helping Izzy's mood.

'I've got a patient on NICU,' Megan explained. 'A new admission. His mum's bipolar and Diego wants some sedation for her. The baby was an emergency transfer so there's no local GP and her medications are all at home. She's getting really agitated, and really it sounds as if she just needs a good night's sleep and then her husband can bring in her meds in the morning. Diego wants her seen straight away, though. Is there any chance? I'd do it but I've *got* to go up to the ward.'

'You'll have to speak to Josh or one of the nurses,' Izzy was unusually terse. 'I'm about to suture someone and then I'm going home.'

She was aware of the rise of Megan's eyebrow. Normally Izzy was accommodating, but Diego's name seemed to be popping up in her day all too often—and her thoughts were turning to him too, rather more than Izzy was comfortable with.

Still it wasn't just a sexy neonatal nurse that had caused Izzy's terse reaction. Just as Jess had predicted, there would be patients that would touch a very raw nerve with Izzy, and even though she had assured Jess she would have no trouble dealing with them, Evelyn Harris *had* hit a nerve.

In her early forties she had presented having tripped over the cat and cut her head on the edge of the coffee table. Vivienne, the student nurse, had had a quiet word with Izzy before she had examined her, telling her that she had noticed some other bruises on her arms when she had checked her blood pressure and, sure enough when Izzy had *checked* the blood pressure again, she had seen the new fingertip bruises, but had chosen not to comment.

'You're going to need a few stitches!' Izzy had said instead. 'How's the cat?'

The relief in the room at Izzy's small joke had been palpable, Evelyn had laughed and John Harris had said the cat would be in the naughty corner, or some other light-hearted thing, and Izzy had smiled back.

Had let him think, as he no doubt did, that she was stupid.

'Vivienne?' Izzy called out to a student nurse. 'Could you set up the minor theatre?' She smiled at

Mrs Harris. 'I'll take you over and I'll be in with you in a moment.'

'I'll stay with you,' Mr Harris reassured his wife, and then explained why to Dumb Doctor Izzy. 'She doesn't like needles.'

'Sorry!' Izzy breezed. 'We can only have the patient.' She gave a very nice smile. 'We shan't be long, at least I hope not. You're my last patient for the night...' She chatted away, not letting the husband get a word in, acted dizzy and vague and rushed, as if getting home was the only thing on her mind, telling them both to take a seat outside minor ops. Then she headed for the annexe, checked who the on-call social worker was for the night and was just considering her options when Megan had asked the favour. With her emotions already bubbling to the surface, the thought of seeing Diego was the last thing she needed.

There was something about him that got under her skin, though in a nice way, and Izzy, right now, just wasn't comfortable with nice.

Wasn't used to nice.

And was nowhere near ready for it either.

As Izzy came into the minor theatre, Vivienne was just bringing Evelyn through and Mr Harris's voice came through the open door as his wife stepped inside.

'I'm right outside, darling,' he said, only Izzy could hear his clear warning.

'Lie down here, Evelyn,' Izzy said, then headed over to the small bench in the corner and turned on the radio. 'Let's have some music to distract you.' She washed her hands and pulled on some gloves and then gently gave the wound a clean before injecting in some local anaesthetic. 'I'm fine on my own, Vivienne,' Izzy said. 'It's pretty busy out there.'

'I'm to cut for you,' came the response, but Izzy could cut her own stitches and wanted to be alone with Evelyn, except Vivienne wouldn't budge. 'Beth told me to get into Theatre as much as I could.'

'Could you get me some 3-0 catgut?' Izzy said, knowing they had run out but checking the wound as if that was the thread she needed. 'There's none here, but I think there should be some in the store cupboard.'

'There isn't any,' Vivienne said. 'I did the stock order with Beth this afternoon.'

Vivienne needed a crash course on taking a hint, but Izzy didn't have time right now. Evelyn only needed a couple of stitches and Mr Harris would no doubt start to get impatient soon, so Izzy dragged the stool over with her foot and given the time constraints realised she would have to be more direct than she would normally choose.

'Evelyn,' Izzy said, 'is there anything you want to tell me?'

'Nothing.'

'I know,' Izzy said gently. 'I know that you didn't just trip…' She watched her patient's nervous lick of her dry lips, her eyes anxiously dart to the theatre door. 'He can't hear,' Izzy said. 'That's why I put the radio on. You can talk to me.'

'Can you just do your job and suture me?' Evelyn bristled. 'I tripped! Okay?'

'There's a bruise on the opposite cheek, finger marks on your arms. I can sort out help...'

'Really?' The single word was so loaded with sarcasm, just so scornful and filled with dark energy that Izzy let out a breath before she spoke next.

'I can ring the social worker. There are shelters...'

'I've a seventeen-year-old son.' Evelyn's lip curled in bitter response. 'The shelters won't let me bring him with me. Did you know that?' she challenged, and Izzy shook her head.

'So what do you suggest, Doctor? That I leave him with him?'

'No, of course not, but if I get someone to speak with you, they could go through your options. I can speak to the police. You don't have to go back tonight.'

'You're not helping, Doctor,' Evelyn said. 'In fact, you could very well be making my life a whole lot worse.'

The stitches took no time, and Izzy knew that dragging it out and keeping Evelyn's husband waiting would only make things worse for her patient, but as Vivienne snipped the last thread Izzy had one more go.

'Is there anyone you can talk to? A friend perhaps...'

'You really don't get it, do you?'

Except Izzy did.

'I don't have *friends*! At least, none of my choosing.'

Evelyn struck a dignified pose as she swung her legs down from the gurney and Izzy recognised the glare in her eyes only too well, because she had shot out that look many times before if anyone had dared so much as to assume that her life was less than perfect.

'Do I need to sign anything?' Evelyn asked.

'No.' Izzy shook her head. 'If you…' She looked at Evelyn and her voice trailed off. Evelyn's decision to stay wasn't going to change, not till her son's future was taken care of. Izzy just hoped to God she'd survive that year. 'When was your last tetanus?'

'I had one…' Evelyn swung her bag over her shoulder '…six weeks ago.'

I'll bet she did, Izzy thought as she stood there, clearing the trolley. She could see her hands shaking as she disposed of the sharps and as Evelyn left Theatre, Izzy had to bite on her lip as the young nurse's disbelieving voice filled the still room.

'Straight back to him…' Her voice was incredulous. 'Why doesn't she just lea—' And then Vivienne's voice abruptly halted as perhaps she remembered who she was talking to and what had had happened the night Izzy had tried to *just* leave.

'She has her reasons,' Izzy said. 'And, frankly, if that's your attitude, she's hardly likely to share them with you.'

'I'm sorry, Izzy.'

And she could have left it there, but Izzy chose not to. Vivienne was thinking of a career in Emergency and, well, it was time she faced a few home truths.

'You're a nurse,' Izzy said, and her voice wobbled with long-held-in emotion, 'not the bloody jury. Remember that when you're dealing with patients in Emergency.'

Her shift was nearly over and all she wanted was out,

so she left the messy trolley and was tempted to just go to the lockers and get out of there. She was angry and close to tears and there was Evelyn walking out of the department, her husband's arm around her. Then he stopped and fished his phone from his jacket and took a call, and Evelyn patiently waited then she turned and for a second. For just a teeny second their eyes locked and and it was the secret handshake, the password, the club, and Evelyn's expression changed as she realised her doctor was a fully paid up member...

'Mrs Harris...' Izzy scribbled down her mobile number on a head injury information chart and walked briskly over. 'Sorry.' Izzy gave a busy shrug. 'I forgot to give you this. Here's your head injury instructions, have a read through...'

'Thank you.'

'And watch out for that cat!' Izzy added, then gave a vague smile at Evelyn and one to her husband before they walked off into the night. Izzy's heart was thumping, not sure what she had just done and not sure what she would even do if Evelyn did call.

She just wanted to do something.

'Izzy!'

That Spanish voice was too nice for her mood right now.

'Can I ask a favour?' Diego gave her a smile as he poked his head out of a cubicle, but she didn't return it.

'I'm about to go off duty.'

'I was off duty forty minutes ago and I'm back on in the morning.' Diego wasn't quite so nice now. One of his mums was about to tip into trouble, the mother of one his precious babies no less. He had spent two hours dealing with red tape, trying to get hold of her GP to fax a prescription, to no avail, or to get a doctor on NICU to see Maria, but of course she wasn't actually a patient at the hospital.

Yet!

Maria was growing more agitated by the minute and no one seemed to give a damn. 'I have a woman who gave birth four days ago, following twenty-four hours of labour. Her child has multiple anomalies, she has hardly slept since her baby was born and she and her husband have driven one hundred miles today as there was no room for them in the helicopter.' Oh, he told her, even if it was Izzy, he told her, even as she opened her mouth to say that she'd see the patient, still he told her, because Diego knew Izzy was far better than that. 'Now she can't settle and is doing her best not to go into meltdown. Can I get a doctor to prescribe me some sedation?'

'I'm sorry, okay?' Izzy's apology was instant and genuine—she had never been one to dash off at the end of her shift, but Evelyn had unsettled her, not to mention Diego. She was having great trouble keeping her mask from slipping, but it wasn't the patients' fault. 'Of course I'll see her.'

Maria was agitated and pacing and the very last thing she needed was endless questions and an examination, and Izzy could see that. Diego had given her a good brief and on gentle questioning Izzy found out what medications the patient was on.

'If I could just get some sleep,' Maria pleaded, and Izzy nodded.

'I'll be back in just a moment.'

She was and so too was a nurse from the neonatal unit to relieve Diego.

'Take two tablets now,' Izzy said, and gave the handover nurse the rest of the bottle. 'She can have two more at two a.m., but don't wake her if she's resting. Will someone be able to check her?'

'Absolutely,' Diego said. 'Maria's staying in the parents' wing, but I'll get my staff to pop in and see her through the night.'

'I'm sure,' Izzy said to her patient, 'that once you've had a decent rest you'll be feeling a lot better. I'm on in the morning,' Izzy added, writing some notes. 'If Maria doesn't settle,' Izzy added to the nurse, 'she'll need to come back down to us.'

It was straightforward and simple and as the nurse took Maria back up to the ward, Diego thanked her.

'I'm sorry if I came on strong.'

'Not at all,' Izzy said. 'She needed to be seen. It's just been a...' She stopped talking; he didn't need to hear about her difficult shift, so she gave him a brief smile and walked on.

Except Diego was going off duty too.

'How's faking it going?' Had he fallen into step beside her that morning, or even an hour ago, Izzy would have managed a laugh and a witty retort, but even a smile seemed like hard work right now, so she just hitched her bag up higher and walked more briskly through the sliding doors and into the ambulance forecourt. But Diego's legs were longer than hers, and he kept up easily.

'Izzy, I was wondering….'

'Do you mind?' She put up her hand to stop him talking, gave an incredulous shake of her head. What was it with people today that they couldn't take a hint if she stood there and semaphored them? 'I just want…' Oh, God, she was going to cry.

Not here.

Not now.

She hadn't yet cried.

Oh, there had been *some* tears, but Izzy had been too scared to really cry, to break down, because if she did, maybe she wouldn't stop.

Scared that if she showed her agony to others they would run when they saw the real her, and scared to do it alone because it was so big, this black, ever-moving shape that had no clear edges, that grew and shrank and transformed.

But she couldn't outrun that black cloud tonight.

She was trying not to cry, trying to breathe and trying to walk away from him to get to her car, as she had tried to that awful night.

No, there was no getting away from it.

Her hands were shaking so much she dropped her keys and it took all her strength not to sink to her knees and break down right there. Instead she got into the car, sat gripping the wheel, holding it in and begging it to pass, but it held her a moment longer, pinning her down. She sat in her car and she was tired, so tired and angry and ashamed and sad…

Sad.

Sad was bigger than angry, bigger than tired, bigger than her.

It was in every cell and it multiplied. It was the membrane of every cell and the nucleus within, it spread and it grew and it consumed and she couldn't escape it any longer. As she doubled over she could feel her baby kick inside and it was so far from the dream, so removed from anything she had envisaged when she had walked down that aisle, that the only word was sad.

She didn't even jump when the passenger door opened and Diego slid into the passenger seat.

'Can't you just leave me alone?'

Diego thought about it for a moment then gave an honest answer. 'It would seem not.'

'You know, don't you?' Izzy said, because everyone else did and so he surely must.

'A little,' Diego admitted. 'I didn't at first, but that morning, when you came to my office, I'd just found out.'

'I thought you were a bit awkward.'

Maybe for a second, Diego thought, but he'd been awkward for another reason that morning, but now wasn't really the time to tell her.

'I've done something stupid...' Izzy said. 'Just then, when you asked me to see Maria.' He sat patiently, waiting for her to explain. 'I had a woman, I think her husband beats her—actually, I don't think, I know. She wouldn't let me help her. I can see now that I rushed in, but I didn't want her to go home to him. I knew what he'd be like when they got home, you could just tell he was annoyed that she was even at the hospital, even though he'd put her there. Anyway, she wouldn't let me get a social worker or the police….' She turned and saw the flash of worry on his face. 'I didn't confront him or anything, he's none the wiser that I know.'

'You can't help her if she doesn't want it.'

'I gave her my phone number.' Izzy waited for his reaction, waited for him to tell her not to get involved, that she had been foolish, but instead he thought for a long moment before commenting.

'I think,' he said slowly, 'that your phone number would be a very nice thing to have.' She blinked. 'And I'm not flirting,' Diego said, and she actually gave a small smile. 'Other times I flirt, but not then. Did *you* talk to anyone?'

'No,' Izzy admitted. 'Megan, we're friends,' she explained, 'asked me what was wrong once, and I remember then that I nearly told her. God—' regret wrapped her words '—I wish I had. I was on my way to my mum's when it happened—I was going to tell her. Henry and I had had a massive row that morning. I knew I was pregnant, that I had to get out of the marriage. I told him I was leaving, I still wasn't sure how, but I came to work, scraped through the shift and afterwards I was going to land on my parents' doorstep…' she gave a shrug '…or Megan's. All I knew was that I wasn't going home.'

'What if someone had given you a phone number?' Diego asked. 'If you had known that that person knew what it was like…'

'I'd have rung them,' Izzy said. 'Not straight away

perhaps.' Then she nodded, confirmed to herself that she hadn't done a stupid thing. 'What do I say if she rings?'

'What would you have wanted someone to say to you?'

'I don't know,' Izzy admitted. 'Just to listen...'

She'd answered her own question and Izzy leant back on the seat and closed her eyes for a moment, actually glad that he had got into the car, glad that he hadn't left her alone, glad that he was there.

And she didn't want to think about it any more so instead she turned to him.

'I forgive you.'

'*Cómo?*' Diego frowned. 'Forgive me for what?'

'Having a satchel.' She watched as a smile spread across his face and she smiled too. 'I never thought I could,' Izzy said, seriously joking, 'but I do.'

'Leave my satchel alone,' Diego said, and he saw something then, her humour, a glimpse of the real Izzy that would soon be unearthed, because she would come out of this, Diego was sure of that. She would grow and she would rise and she would become more of the woman he was glimpsing now.

He knew.

And he knew if he stayed another minute he'd kiss her.

'I'd better go,' Diego said, because he really thought he'd better.

'I'll drive you.'

'No, because then I would have to ask you in.'

'Would that be so bad?' Izzy asked, because it felt as

if he was kissing her, she could see his mouth and almost taste it on hers. Sitting in the car, she didn't want him to get out and she didn't want to drive on. She wanted to stay in this moment, but Diego was moving them along.

'If you come in, I might not want you to leave...' It was big and it was unexpected and the last thing either had planned for, yet, ready or not, it was happening. 'We need to think.'

He climbed out of her car and Izzy sat there. Without him beside her logic seeped in.

It was way too soon.

It was impossibly way too soon.

And yet, had he chosen to, he could have kissed her.

CHAPTER SIX

Qué diablos estás haciendo?

As Diego pushed through the waves, over and over he asked himself what on earth he was doing.

On leaving Izzy, he'd gone home to find Sally in the car outside his flat, with a bottle of wine and a dazzling smile, but instead of asking her in, he'd sent her on her way. The words 'It's been good, but…' had hung in the air, as had the sound of her tears, but it had been the only outcome to their relationship, Diego had realised as he'd let himself into his flat.

It *had* been good.

Sencillo, Diego's favourite word—straightforward, uncomplicated. Sally had been all those things and everything Diego had thought he wanted in a relationship. Only his life had suddenly become a touch more complicated.

He needed to think and he couldn't do that with Sally. Wouldn't do that to Sally and also he needed to be very sure himself.

Walking out of the water towards the beach, he wasn't sure if he was even pleased that Izzy had taken his advice, for there she was, walking along the beach, her face flushing when she saw him.

'I thought you were on an early…'

'I'm on a management day, so I don't have to be in till nine,' Diego explained, then he teased, 'Why? Were you trying to avoid me?'

'Of course not!' Izzy lied.

'It's good to see you out.'

'It's good to be out,' Izzy admitted. 'I used to walk on the beach each morning. I don't know why I stopped.'

'You've had a lot to deal with.'

Which she had, but Izzy hadn't walked since her marriage, another little thing she'd given up in an attempt to please Henry, but she didn't say anything.

'Do you want company?'

And she looked into dark eyes that were squinting against the morning sun, his black hair dripping, unshaven, wet, and his toned body, way smoother than a name like Ramirez suggested, and she didn't know what she wanted because, here was the thing, she'd spent the whole night in turmoil, telling herself she was being ridiculous, that it was impossible, that she should be sorting out herself instead of getting involved with someone.

She didn't actually have to tell herself. The books said the same too, even Jess.

But here, on the beach, when she should be thinking alone, it was his company her heart required. Here in the lovely fresh start of morning it just seemed natural for them to talk.

They walked along the beach, admiring the rugged

Cornish coastline. Despite the warmth of summer, the wind was up, making the beach the coolest place as the breeze skimmed off the ocean and stung her cheeks, and it was a relief to talk about him.

'This beach is one of the reasons I choose to settle in St Piran. I love the beach.'

'What about Madrid? Do you miss it?'

'The nearest beach is Valencia. Over a hundred miles away...' Perhaps he realised he was being evasive. 'Sometimes I miss it. I have been away two years now...' She glanced at him when his voice trailed off.

'Go on.'

'My family and I were rowing—we did not part on good terms,' Diego admitted. 'We get on a bit better now. I talk to my mother often on the telephone, but for a while there was no contact.'

He left it there, for now. But there was something about the ocean. It was so vast and endless that it made honesty easier, problems mere specks, which was perhaps why they found themselves there so often over the next few days. They would walk and talk and try to put on hold the chemistry between them and instead work on their history. They sat in the shallows, just enough for the cool water to wash around their ankles and up their calves, and they talked. It was absolutely, for Izzy, the best part of her day and she hoped Diego felt the same.

'I told you it was expected that I would study medicine? It did not go down well when I chose to study nursing instead. Padre said it was women's work...'

'Not any more.'

'He ridiculed it, my brothers too. I also studied *parte-ro*, I'm a midwife too,' Diego explained. 'My mother said she understood, but she would prefer I study medicine to keep my father happy.' He gave a wry smile. 'That was the rule growing up and it is still the rule now—keeping him happy. Getting good grades, melting into the background, anything to keep him happy. I wish she had the guts to leave him.' He looked over at Izzy. 'I admire you for leaving.'

'I didn't have children,' Izzy said. 'And it was still a hard decision. Don't judge her for staying, Diego. What made you want to do nursing?'

'My elder sister had a baby when I was eighteen. He was very premature and my sister was ill afterwards. I used to sit with him and I watched the nurses. They were so skilled, so much more hands on than the doctors, and I knew it was what I wanted to do. Fernando was very sick—I was there night and day for ten days. My sister had a hysterectomy and was very sick too…' There was a long silence. 'She was at another hospital so she didn't get over to see him—she was too ill.' Diego suddenly grimaced. 'I shouldn't be telling you this…'

'I'm not that precious.' Izzy squeezed his hand.

'He died at ten days old. It was tough. In those ten days I really did love him and even now sometimes my sister asks for details about him and I am glad that I can give them to her.'

'What sort of details?'

'He loved to have his feet stroked and he loved to be sing to.' He gave a slight frown and Izzy just sat silent rather than correct his grammar. 'My sister had always sung to him while she was pregnant and I taped her singing and played the songs.'

'It must be hard,' Izzy said. 'Your work must bring it all back...'

'No.' His response surprised her. 'It has certainly made me a better nurse. I know, as much as I can know, how helpless and scared the parents feel. How you constantly watch the monitors and become an armchair expert, but never, not even once, have I come close to the feelings I had for Fernando with a patient. I suppose I detach, of course there are stories and babies that touch you more than others, but you could not do this job and care so deeply at that level.'

And she looked at him and couldn't see how his parents could be anything but proud. She had seen his work at first hand, the way his colleagues and all the parents respected him. There had been an almost audible sigh of relief that Diego had been around when Toby had been born and she told him that.

'There is a managerial position at my father's hospital—I am thinking of applying for it. Of course, it has not gone down well. He says it would be an embarrassment to the Ramirez name if I take it.'

They were only just getting to know each other, but still her breath caught at the impossibility of it all, of anything happening between them, and she tried to keep the needy note from her voice when she asked a question.

'Why would you go back?' Izzy asked, 'After all that, if they don't respect what you do...'

'I respect what I do now,' Diego said. 'That is the difference. I would like to go back and be proud.'

He would go back.

They were sitting in the sand at the water's edge. Izzy's shorts were soaking, the water rushing in then dragging back out, as if taking all the debris of the past away. But the tide returned and bought with it fresh problems and Izzy told herself to slow down, to not even think about it, that his decisions didn't affect her. They were friends, that was all—they hadn't so much as kissed.

Except Diego discounted that theory before it had even properly formed.

She could feel his face near her cheek and knew if she turned her head their lips would meet.

It was six a.m. and the clearest her head would be all day, but she turned to him, to the sweet, confusing relief of his mouth. He tasted like a blast of morning, with the promise of night. It was a kiss that was tender on the outside—a mesh of lips, a slow, measured greeting, but there was raw promise beneath the surface, his tongue sliding in, offering a heady taste of more, and Izzy wanted more. She liked the press of him, the weight of him that pressed her body back to the sand. There was the tranquillity of escape she found as his kiss deepened and his hand moved naturally, sliding around her waist to caress her, and then even before Diego paused, Izzy's lips were still.

She rested her head on his shoulder a moment to steady herself, the weight of her baby between them.

'I think...' Izzy pulled her head up and made

herself look at him '...we should pretend that just didn't happen.'

'It did, though,' Diego pointed out.

'Well, it can't again,' Izzy said, and she hoisted herself to standing. 'Let's just keep it as friends,' Izzy insisted, because that was surely all they could be for now, except her lips were tender from the claim of his kiss as she tried to talk about *other* things, and as they walked back her hand bunched in a fist so she didn't reach out and take his.

They were back at her car, his apartment just a short walk away, and how he wanted to take her up there, to peel off her wet clothes and call in sick, spend the day getting to know her in the way he so badly wanted to.

And friends could kiss goodbye on the cheek, except they had passed that now and any contact between them was dangerous.

He faced her, but that only made him want to kiss her again so Diego looked down and saw the swell of her stomach, her belly button just starting to protrude, and his hand ached to capture it, only his mind wasn't so sure.

'We have a lot to think about,' Diego said, 'or maybe it's better not to think about it, just...' He looked up at her and his face was honest and it scared her, but somehow it made her smile as he offered her a very grown-up slant on words said in playgrounds the world over. 'I don't want to be your friend any more.'

CHAPTER SEVEN

'YOU'RE expected to go, Diego!' Rita was adamant. 'You can't not go to the Penhally Ball.'

They'd been having this conversation all morning. Rita had found out that he wasn't going and it seemed every time he passed her work station, she thought of another reason why he must go.

He'd just come from a family meeting with the parents of Toby Geller, which had been difficult at best, and, really, the last thing Diego cared about was if he was *expected* to attend some charity ball that was being held on Saturday.

'You're going, aren't you, Megan?' Rita looked up and Diego rolled his eyes as Megan gave a thin smile.

'It is expected,' Megan agreed, but from her resigned voice it was clear she wasn't looking forward to it.

'All the units send their senior staff,' Rita said, still talking as she answered the phone.

'Spare me,' Diego said. 'Is it awful?'

'No.' Megan shook her head. 'It's actually a great night...'

'So why the long face?' He was friends with Megan.

Well, not 'ring each other up every night and why don't we go for coffee type friends', but certainly they were friendly and Diego couldn't help but notice she was unusually low.

'Just one of those days!' Megan said, which given they had just been in with Toby's parents, could have explained it, except Megan hadn't been her usual self lately. Diego suddenly wondered if it had anything to do with the rumours that were flying around the hospital about Izzy and himself.

Diego hadn't realised just how many people he knew. And Izzy too.

It seemed that everywhere they went, be it a walk on the beach or to a café near his flat, they would bump into someone from work. But it wasn't just the rumour mill causing problems. Izzy was almost nine weeks from her due date now, and despite them both trying to be nothing more than just friends, that kiss had unleashed the attraction between them. It was so palpable, so present, it was killing Diego not to whisk her away from the home she was selling and bring her back to his flat, feed her, nurture her and make love to her. Except in a few weeks' time, Izzy would be a mother, which meant there would be a baby, and that was something way down on his list.

So far down, he hadn't actually thought whether one day he might want one of his own—let alone someone else's.

But he wanted her.

'It's a lovely night.' Rita just wouldn't let up; she was off the phone and back to one of her favourite subjects—prying about Megan. 'All the money raised goes to the Penhally Rape Crisis Centre. Will you be taking anyone, Doctor?'

Ah, but Megan was always one step ahead. 'You heard the man.' Megan flashed Rita a smile that was false. 'He doesn't want to go.'

'Oh!'

Diego couldn't help but grin as a Rita's eyes momentarily widened as she wondered if she'd stumbled on the news of year, but then she remembered the latest information from her sources. She turned back to the computer and resumed typing. Attempting nonchalance, she tested the seemingly gentle waters. 'It's good to support these things.' Rita tap tapped away, 'Look what happened to our own lovely Izzy. I'd have thought you, Diego, more than anyone, would...' And she stopped, just stopped in mid-sentence, because even if she wasn't looking at him, even if Diego hadn't spoken, the atmosphere was so tense, she just knew he wasn't smiling now. 'We should all do our bit,' Rita attempted, typing faster now, hoping she'd rectified it, and hoping Diego hadn't understood what she had implied.

She was wrong on both counts.

'Me? More? Than? Anyone?' Diego's voice was pure ice as he challenged her—each word separate, each word a question, and Diego looked at Megan, who shook her head in disbelief at Rita's insensitivity. 'What do you mean by that, Rita?'

Still she typed on. 'Well, you're a nice young man, I thought you of all people...' Her face was pink and she licked her lips before carrying on. 'Well, that you'd support such a thing.'

'Do you know why I hate gossip, Megan?' Diego looked at his friend.

'Why?' Megan answered.

'Because the fools that spread it get it wrong. Because the fools that spread it are so miserable in their own lives they have to find that part in others...' Rita stood up.

'I have to get on.' She picked up some papers, *any* papers, and walked off, but Diego's voice chased her.

'Because though they insist their lives are perfect, gossiping about others ensures that for that moment no one is gossiping about them.'

Rita spun on her heel. 'You can't stop people talking.'

'Ah, but you can,' Diego said, and pointedly turned to Megan, ignoring Rita completely. 'Before you go, I've got two in the nursery that need their drug charts re-written and Genevieve is ready to go home. Her mum wants to thank you.'

It was a relief to talk about work.

For Megan to fill in the drug charts and then to head to the nursery where Genevieve was wearing a hot pink all-in-one with a hot pink hat, and a car seat was waiting to finally, against all the odds, take her home. Diego smiled as Megan picked up the little lady and gave her a cuddle, and he could see the tears in her eyes too because, unlike Diego, Megan did get attached. She gave her heart and soul to her patients, took it personally when a battle was lost. Diego wasn't sure it was a healthy thing for her to do, but today was a good day and those, Diego suddenly realised, were the ones Megan struggled with most.

'We can't thank you enough.' Genevieve's mum was effusive in her gratitude. 'It's because of you that we get to take her home.'

Yes, today was a good day.

'Good job,' Diego said before he headed back to his charges. 'For a while there I didn't think we'd get to this day with Genevieve. You never gave in, though.'

'I never would,' Megan said, and then she paused and her voice was more pensive than jubilant. 'Be careful, Diego.'

He knew exactly what they were talking about.

'We're just friends,' he said, but he could hear the protest in his heart and Megan could hear it in his voice.

'She's fragile…'

'She's getting stronger,' Diego countered, because he would not label Izzy, because he could feel in his soul all she was going to be.

'Just, please,' Megan said, and it was the most she would say to him, 'handle with care.'

'You're looking well.' Gus smiled as he called Izzy into his surgery.

He was a wonderful GP. He read through her charts and checked her blood pressure, even though the midwife had done the same and told Izzy it was fine.

'How is it?'

'Perfect,' Gus said. 'How have you been feeling?'

'Very well,' Izzy said, and it was the truth. For the first time in her pregnancy it wasn't Henry and the nightmare of her past that consumed her, it was something far nicer.

There had been no repeat of that kiss, but there was an energy and promise in her days now and Izzy knew it was just a matter of time.

'You're eating well?' Gus checked, and though his face never flickered, Izzy was a doctor too and could hear the slight probing nature of his question. Often her antenatal visits seemed more like a friendly catch-up, but today Gus was going through her notes, double-checking everything.

'I'm eating really well.' Which was true. In the very dark weeks after Henry's death, even though eating had been the last thing on her mind, Izzy had made herself eat, for the baby's sake. She had even gone as far as to set a reminder on her mobile, forcing down smoothies or even just a piece of toast. But since she'd been back at work, and of course since she'd met Diego, her appetite had returned—for food, for life. She was laughing, she was happy, she was eating—except her weight, Gus said, was down.

It seemed ironic that when she was eating the most, when she was happiest, she hadn't put on any weight. Gus asked her to lie on the examination bed, and though he was always thorough, today his examination took a little longer than usual.

'You're a bit small,' Gus said, and Izzy lay there staring at the ceiling, because if Gus said she was a bit small, then she *was* small. He ran a Doppler over her stomach and listened for a couple of moments to the baby's heartbeat, which was strong and regular. 'How's the baby's movement?'

'There's lots,' Izzy said, trying to keep her voice light and even.

'That's good.' He was very calm, very unruffled and he helped her sit up and then she joined him at his desk.

'Are you worried?' Izzy asked.

'Not unduly,' Gus said. 'Izzy, you've had unbelievable stress throughout this pregnancy—but you're thirty-one weeks now and this is the time that the baby starts to put on weight, so we really do need to keep a slightly closer eye on you. I was going to schedule an ultrasound for a couple of weeks, but let's bring that forward.' He glanced at his watch. It was six on Friday evening. 'Let's get this done early next week and then…' She was due to start coming to fortnightly visits now, but Gus was nothing if not thorough. 'Let's get the scan and I'll see you again next week.'

'You know that I'm working?' Izzy felt incredibly guilty, but Gus moved to reassure her.

'Lots of my mums work right up till their due date, Izzy. You're doing nothing wrong—for now. I just want you to try and reduce your stress and really make sure you're eating well. You need some extra calories. I'd suggest you add a protein shake to your breakfast.'

'I'm supposed to be going to the Penhally Ball tomorrow…'

Out of the blue Diego had suggested they go together— face the gossip and just get it over and done with, and what better way than at the Penhally Ball, when everyone would be there. They had, Diego had pointed out, absolutely nothing to be ashamed of. To the world they were friends and friends went out! Except Izzy still cared what others might think and almost hoped Gus would shake his head and tell her that the weekend might be better spent resting on the couch with her feet up, thus give her a reason not to go, but Gus seemed delighted. 'That's good—I'm glad you're starting to go out.'

'Shouldn't I be resting?'

'Izzy, I'm not prescribing bed rest—I want you to relax and a social life is a part of that. I just want to keep a closer eye on you.'

'The thing is...' She was testing the water, just dipping in her toe. She respected Gus, and his reaction mattered. 'Things have been awful, but for the last few weeks, for the first time since I've been pregnant, I haven't had any stress or, rather, much less, and I have been eating better...'

'Well, whatever it is you're doing, keep it up,' Gus said, and Izzy gave a small swallow.

'I'm going to the ball with a friend, Diego.'

'Ramirez.' Izzy frowned as Gus said his surname.

'You know him?'

'There aren't too many Diegos around here. The neonatal nurse?'

And she waited for his shock-horror reaction, for him to tell her she should be concentrating on the baby now, not out dancing with male *friends*, but instead Gus smiled.

'He seems a nice man.'

When Izzy just sat there Gus smiled. 'You deserve nice, Izzy.'

She still didn't know it.

CHAPTER EIGHT

SHE'D cancel.

Izzy could hardly hear the hairdresser's comments as she sat with a black cape around her shoulders, pretending to look as a mirror was flashed behind her head.

'It looks fantastic!'

Well, she would say that, Izzy thought to herself. The hairdresser was hardly going to say, 'It looks awful and what on earth were you thinking, taking a pair of scissors to your locks, you stupid tart?' But as the mirror hovered behind her Izzy actually did look, and for once she agreed with the woman who wielded the scissors.

Okay, maybe fantastic was stretching things a touch, but it had been three months and three trips to this chair since that moment of self-loathing and finally, finally, she didn't look like a five-year-old who had taken the kitchen scissors to the bathroom. The last of her home-made crop had been harvested, the once jagged spikes now softened, shades of blonde and caramel moving when her head did, which it did as Izzy craned her neck for a proper look.

'I've hardly taken anything off at the front or sides,

just softened it a touch, but I've taken a fair bit off the back…'

Izzy could have kissed her but instead she left a massive tip, booked in for six weeks' time, skipped out to her car and somehow made it home without incident, despite the constant peeks in the rear-view mirror at her very new 'side fringe'.

And then she remembered.

She was cancelling.

So why was she running a bath and getting undressed?

A tepid bath so it didn't fluff up her hair.

She couldn't do it, couldn't go, just couldn't face it.

So instead of climbing in to the water she wrapped herself in a towel and padded out to the living room.

She had every reason to cancel, Izzy told herself as she picked up the telephone, except there was a voice-mail message. It wasn't Diego stuck at work, as she had rather hoped, but the real estate agent with a pathetic offer. 'It's a good offer, you should seriously consider it,' played the message. Henry had been a real estate agent and had practically said those words in his sleep so she deleted it and got back to fretting about Diego. The fact that she was pregnant and had worked all morning, the fact that she wasn't ready for the inevitable stares if she walked into the Penhally Ball with a dashing Spaniard on her arm when she should be home…

Doing what? Izzy asked herself.

Grieving, feeling wretched…

Her introspection was halted by the doorbell. No doubt the postman had been while she was out and it was her neighbour with another box of self-help or baby books that she had ordered on the internet during one of her glum times—a book that at the time she had convinced herself would be the one to show her, tell her, inform her how the hell she was supposed to be feeling...

'Diego?'

It was only five p.m. and he shouldn't be there, the ball didn't start till seven.

There was no reason for him to be there now and, worse, she was only wearing a towel.

'I thought I'd come early.' He leant in the doorway and smiled, and either the baby did a big flip or her stomach curled in on itself. He was in evening wear, except he hadn't shaved, and he looked ravishing, so ravishing she wanted to do just that—ravish him, drop the towel she was clinging to, right here at the front door. 'To save you that phone call.'

'What phone call?' Izzy lowered her head a touch as she let him in, wishing there had been a warning sign on the kitchen scissors to inform her that it would be a full twelve to eighteen months before she could again hide her facial expressions with her hair if she chose to lop it all off. A fringe simply wouldn't suffice. Her whole body was on fire, every pulse leaping at the sight of him.

'The one where you tell me your back is aching, or you're tired or that it was lovely of me to ask, but...'

'I was just about to make it,' Izzy admitted.

'Why?'

'Because it's too soon.'

'For what?'

'For me to be out, for me to be...' She blanched at the unsaid word.

'Happy?' Diego offered. 'Living?'

Neither was quite right. Izzy didn't correct him at first, she just clung to her towel, not to keep him from her but to keep her from him, and she stared at a man who had brought nothing but joy into her life. She wanted more of the same.

'For me to be seeing someone,' Izzy corrected. 'Which I think I am.'

'You are,' he confirmed, and crossed the room. It was a relief to be kissed, to kiss him, to be kissed some more, to kiss back. He was less than subtle, he was devouring her, and any vision that their next kiss would be gentle and tender was far removed from delicious reality. Diego had waited long for another kiss and he was claiming it now, pressing her against the wall as she rejoiced in him, her towel falling. He kicked it away and all she wanted was more, more, more.

He tasted as he had that morning but decisiveness made it better. He smelt as he always had, just more concentrated now, and this close to Diego, this into Diego, she forgot to be scared and hold back.

Izzy just forgot.

She could have climbed up the wall and slid onto him he felt so delicious, but just as her senses faded to oblivion, Diego resurrected one of his.

'Is that a bath?'

Now, this bit she didn't get.

Sense *should* have prevailed.

In her mad dash to turn off the taps, okay, yes it was okay that he followed, but then, *then* she should have shown him the door, should have closed it on him and had a few moments' pause, except she let him help her into the bath and then she remembered to be practical. 'Diego, we can't.'

'I know.' He took off his jacket, hung it on the doorhandle and then sat on the edge and looked at her, and she couldn't believe how normal it felt.

'We can't,' he confirmed, because of the baby she carried. 'How far along are you again?' He grinned and then rolled his eyes as he did the mental arithmetic, because this thing between them had already been going on for a couple of weeks!

'Poor Diego.' Why was she laughing? Lying in the bath and laughing like she was happy. And the fact that she was made her suddenly serious.

'How can this work—ever?' Izzy asked, because surely it was impossible. 'You're going back to Spain.'

'Nope.' He shook his head. 'I didn't apply.'

'There'll be other jobs though. One day you will go back.' And he couldn't argue with that, so instead she watched as he rolled up his sleeves and two tanned olive hands took a lilac bar of soap and worked it. She could see the bubbles between his fingers, see the moist, slippery sheen of his hands, and her body quivered and begged for them to be on her. As his hands met her shoulders her mind stopped looking for reasons to halt this and her brain stopped begging for logic and all she did was feel—feel his strong fingers on her tense shoulders, feel the knots of tight muscles spasm in momentary protest as this large Spaniard had the nerve to tell them to let go. For months, no, maybe a year, or had it been longer, those muscles had been knotted with the serious job of holding her head up high and now they were being told to let go, to give in, that they could relax, regroup and get ready for the next mountain Izzy was certain that she would surely have to climb. But Diego's hands worked on and convinced her shoulders, if not her mind, to do as the master skilfully commanded, and let go.

Her fringe almost met the water with the relief.

Like popping a balloon she just gave in, just groaned as her tension seeped into the water and then steamed out into the room.

She just couldn't let go for long, though.

'I can't get my hair wet!' She flailed at all his hands were offering, she just couldn't relax and enjoy it in long stages. 'How can this work, Diego?' she asked again.

'*Sencillo*,' Diego said, 'It doesn't have to be complicated. Why not just for now? Why not for as long as we make each other happy?'

'Because in nine weeks I'll be diving into postnatal depression and I won't be making anyone happy!'

She wanted guarantees.

Wanted a little piece of paper stamped with *I won't hurt you* to be handed to her now, except she'd had that once, Izzy realised as she lay there, a big piece of paper called a wedding certificate, and it hadn't counted for a thing.

Before Diego had come along living had been like essential surgery without analgesia.

Why would she deny herself the balm of relief?

And there was a wobble of guilt there, but for him. 'What if I'm using you!' God, she had never been so honest, and certainly not with a man. All her relationships had been Izzy pleasing others, Izzy saying the right thing, and now here she was, ten minutes into a new one and saying the wrong thing, saying truthfully what was on her mind. 'What if I'm using you to get through this?'

And he thought about it for a moment, he actually did, and then he came to his decision.

'Use away!'

'What if I'm avoiding my pain by...?'

'Shut up.' He grinned and leaned over and kissed her a nice lazy kiss. Then he kissed her shoulder and along the slippery wet lines of her neck.

Oh, Diego loved women. He loved curves on women and two of Izzy's were floating on the water, just bobbing there, and his hands moved to her shoulders, because it seemed more polite. But then his hands just moved to where they wanted to be and he caressed them, caressed her. His big, dark hands cupped and soaped her very white, rather large, to Izzy rather ugly breasts, but maybe they weren't so ugly, because from the trip in his breathing and the bob of his tongue on his dark lips, she had the feeling that one tug of his tie and he'd be in the water with her, and there would be two empty seats at the Penhally Charity Ball.

'We can't,' she said again and it was the feeblest of protests, because the stubble of his chin was scratching her breast now, his tongue on her nipple and her fingers in his hair.

'You can,' Diego said, as his hand slid beneath the water.

She never fully forgot about the hell of the past months and years. No matter how good, how happy, how busy she was, no matter what conversation she was holding, it never completely left her mind, but as his hand slid beneath the water and Izzy could feel his fingers at the top of her thighs, ever-present thoughts started to fade. She could feel his hot mouth on her cool shoulder and always, always, always she had thought of pleasing *him*, not Diego, but *him*, and the mute button hit and there was nothing to think of but this, nothing to relish but Diego's tender explorations as she wriggled in his palm.

Her cynical voice gave one last call for order. After all, she didn't come with instructions, and he must do this an awful lot, because his fingers read her so well, but she was kissing his neck and above his white collar, coiling her wet fingers in his dark hair as a heavenly regular pressure beat beneath the water. And suddenly she didn't care if he did this a lot, he was doing it to her, right now, and he could go on doing it for ever, it was so divine. He stroked her back to life, cajoled her hibernating clitoris from its dreamless sleep, and it stretched and peeked out and Izzy was sure this feeling must end, that she'd shift or he'd pause and that the magic would stop, and she didn't want it to.

She couldn't lean back because she didn't want to.

She couldn't reach for the sides of the bath because then she couldn't hold him.

She held his shirt-clad back with wet arms and

muffled her face in his neck and beneath the cologne that he was wearing tonight was the true scent of him, the one that every cell in her body had flared for on sight and burnt now with direct contact.

Let go, his fingers insisted. *Let go*, the stubble of his chin told her eyelids as she pressed her face into him. She could hear the lap, lap, lap of the water and the patience yet relentlessness of him and she did as his fingers told her, she didn't know what she said and she didn't know what she did—she just let go. She was almost climbing out of the bath and into his arms, but he held her down and it was so much better than being just friends. And as she opened her eyes he closed his; as he struggled to get through the next nine seconds, Izzy was wondering how they'd get through the next nine weeks. She wanted more of him.

'We're going to be late.' He was trying to sound normal.

Really, really late, because Izzy now had to sort out her hair and do her make-up *and* show him where the ironing board was so he could iron his shirt dry.

But it was more than worth it.

CHAPTER NINE

SHE had known heads would turn and they did, but what Izzy hadn't expected were the smiles that followed the arches of the eyebrows as they walked in together.

Real smiles, because how could they not?

Izzy had been through so very much and her friends and colleagues had been worried about her, had not known how to react in the face of such raw pain and grief, but tonight she was glowing and it wasn't just from the pregnancy.

'Don't you dare say you're just friends, because I won't believe you.' Megan came over as Diego went to the bar. 'Friends,' Megan said, 'are able to go two minutes without eye contact,' she pointed out as she caught Izzy and Diego share a lingering look from across the room. 'Friends don't light up a room with their energy when they walk in. Friends don't cause every head to turn. Friends, my foot…' Megan laughed.

'Okay, 'Izzy said, and though it was all a bit like a runaway train, she felt exhilarated as she rode it, smiled as she said it: 'We're more than friends.'

'Happy?' Megan checked.

'Very.'

'Then I'm happy for you,' Megan said. Izzy was sure she would have loved to have said more, but sometimes good friends didn't. Sometimes good friends had to let you make your own success or mistakes and be there for you whatever the outcome. Megan confirmed that with her next words.

'I'm always here.'

'I know that.'

'So how did you manage the night off? I thought you were on.'

'No.' Izzy shook her head, 'I told you, I'm only doing days till the baby's born. I thought you were on call?'

'Richard didn't want to come to the ball, so he's covering for me,' Megan said. 'So who's holding the fort in A and E tonight?'

'Mitch,' Izzy said.

'He's only a resident.'

'Oh, Ben is on call, said he might pop in if he can get away....' And her voice trailed off, because Izzy realised then that Megan hadn't actually been enquiring about her roster, she had been fishing to find out the whereabouts of someone else. And as Megan stood and kissed Izzy on the cheek and headed off into the throng of people, Izzy found a corner of an unexpected jigsaw.

She could see Megan, her usually pale cheeks, suddenly flushed and pink, desperately trying to focus on a conversation, but her green eyes kept flicking over to Josh. It was as if there were an invisible thread between them, a thread that tightened. She watched as

Josh worked the room, each greeting, each two-minute conversation seemed to be dragging him on a human Mexican wave towards Megan. The pull was so strong, Izzy could have sworn she could have reached out and grabbed it.

And then it snapped.

Izzy watched as a blonde woman walked over, all smiles, and kissed Josh possessively on the lips. Izzy saw the wedding band glint on her finger and as Megan's face turned away, Izzy knew Megan had just seen it too.

'Excuse me...' All the colour had drained out of Megan's face and she walked quickly to the ladies. Izzy looked over at Josh who was concentrating on something his wife was saying, but then he caught her eye and Izzy couldn't read his expression, but something told her it was a plea to help.

'Here...' Diego was back with the drinks and it was Izzy's turn to excuse herself, but by the time she got to the ladies Megan was on her way out.

'Hey?' Izzy smiled. 'Are you okay?'

'I'm great!' Megan gave a dazzling smile. 'It's always a good night.'

'Megan?' Izzy caught her friend's arm, but Megan shook it off.

'I must get back out there.'

Oh, she wanted to know what was going on, to help, to fix, to share, only it was clear all Megan wanted to do was to get through this night.

'Sit with us,' Izzy suggested. 'I thought we would be with the emergency guys and girls or NICU, but we left the booking too late and we're with the maternity mob. Come and keep us company.' It was the best she could do for Megan right now and when Megan jumped at the suggestion, Izzy knew she had been right.

There was something going on with Megan and Josh.

Or, Izzy pondered, there had been.

It was actually a good night—the food was wonderful, the company great. Diego was clearly a hit with the maternity team as well, but as the table was cleared and the dancing commenced Izzy was uncomfortable all of a sudden in the hard chair. Stretching her spine, she shifted her weight and she was glad to stretch her legs when Diego asked her to dance.

It was such bliss to be in his arms.

To smell him, to be held by him.

She wished the music would last for ever—that somehow she could freeze this moment of time, where there was no past to run from and no future that could change things. She wished she could dance and dance, just hold this moment and forever feel his breath on her neck and his warm hands on her back, to feel the bulge of her pregnant stomach pressed to his and to remember...

She was dizzy almost remembering a couple of hours earlier.

'Glad you came?' Diego asked.

'Very,' Izzy said, and then pulled back and smiled. 'And more than a little surprised that I did.'

Every day he saw another side to her.

Diego was far from stupid. Of course he had questioned the wisdom of getting involved with someone at such a vulnerable time—fatherhood was not on his agenda. After a lifetime of rules and the stuffy confines of his family, he had sworn it would be years before anyone or anything pinned him down. He was devoted to his work and everything else was just a pleasure, but now, holding her in his arms, life was starting to look a little different.

'Hey.' He'd sensed her distraction. 'What are you watching?'

'What's going on,' she asked, 'with Megan and Josh?'

Diego rolled his eyes. 'Not you too? Rita, my ward clerk, is obsessed with them.'

'Megan's been different lately,' Izzy insisted. 'Surely you've noticed?'

'I've had my mind on other things,' he said, pulling her in a little tighter. 'There's nothing going on,' Diego said assuredly, and glanced at the subjects of their conversation. 'They're not even talking to each other.'

Which was such a male thing to say, but Megan was right, Izzy thought, watching Josh's eyes scan the room as he danced with his wife, watched them locate and capture and hold their target, almost in apology, until Megan tore hers away.

Friends don't share looks like that.

But in that moment all thoughts of Josh and Megan faded, all thoughts of Diego and romance too, because the back pain she had felt while sitting returned, spreading out from her spine like two large hands, stretching around to her stomach and squeezing. It wasn't a pain as such, she'd been having Braxton-Hicks' contractions, but this felt different, tighter. This didn't take her breath, neither did it stop her swaying in the darkness with Diego, but she was more than aware of it and then it was gone and she tried to forget that it had happened. only Diego had been aware of it too.

He had felt her stomach, which was pressed into his, tighten.

He didn't want to be one of those paranoid people. She was just dancing on so he did too, but he was almost more aware of her body than his own. He could feel the slight shift and knew that even though she danced on and held him, her mind was no longer there.

'You okay?'

'Great,' she murmured, hoping and praying that she was. The music played on and Diego suggested that they sit this next one out. Izzy was about to agree, only suddenly the walk back to their table seemed rather long. The music tipped into the next ballad and Izzy leant on him as the next small wave hit, only this time it did make her catch her breath and Diego could pretend no more.

'Izzy?' She heard the question in his voice.

'I don't know,' she admitted. 'Can you get me outside?' she said, still leaning on him, waiting for it to pass. 'In a moment.'

Their exit was discreet. He had a hand round her waist and they didn't stop to get her bag, and as the cool night air hit, Izzy wondered if she was overreacting because now she felt completely normal.

'Izzy.' Discreet as their exit had been, Gus must have

noticed because he joined them outside, just as another contraction hit.

'They're not strong,' Izzy said as Gus placed a skilled hand on her abdomen.

'How far apart?' Gus asked, and it was Diego who answered.

'Six, maybe seven minutes.'

'Okay.' Gus wasted no time. 'Let's get you over to the hospital and we can pop you on a monitor. I'll bring the Jeep around.'

'Should we call an ambulance?' Diego asked, but Gus shook his head.

'We'll be quicker in my Jeep and if we have to pull over, I've got everything we need.'

'I'm not having it,' Izzy insisted, only neither Diego nor Gus was convinced.

It was a thirty-minute drive from Penhally. Diego felt a wave of unease as Izzy's hand gripped his tighter and she blew out a long breath. He remembered his time on Maternity and often so often it was a false alarm, the midwives could tell. Izzy kept insisting she was fine, that the contractions weren't that bad, but he could feel her fingers digging into his palms at closer intervals, could see Gus glancing in the rear-view mirror when Izzy held her breath every now and then, and the slight acceleration as Gus drove faster.

His mind was racing, awful scenarios playing out, but Izzy could never have guessed. He stayed strong and supportive beside her, held her increasingly tightening fingers as Gus rang through and warned the hospital of their arrival. A staff member was waiting with a wheelchair as they pulled up at the maternity section.

'It's too soon,' Izzy said as he helped her out of the Jeep.

'You're in the right place,' Diego said, only he could feel his heart hammering in his chest, feel the adrenaline coursing through him as she was whisked off and all he could do was give her details as best as he could to a new night receptionist.

'You're the father?' ahe asked, and his lips tightened as he shook his head, and he felt the relegation.

'I'm a friend,' Diego said. 'Her...' But he didn't know what to follow it up with. It had been just a few short weeks, and he wasn't in the least surprised when he was asked to take a seat in a bland waiting room

He waited, unsure what to do, what his role was—if he even had a role here.

Going over and over the night, stunned at how quickly everything had changed. One minute they had been dancing, laughing—now they were at the hospital.

The logical side of his brain told him that thirty-one weeks' gestation was okay. Over and over he tried to console himself, tried to picture his reaction if he knew a woman was labouring and he was preparing a cot to receive the baby. Yet there was nothing logical about the panic that gripped him when he thought of Izzy's baby being born at thirty-one weeks. Every complication, every possibility played over and over. It was way too soon, and even if everything did go well, Izzy would be in for a hellish ride when she surely didn't deserve it.

They could stop the labour, though. Diego swung

between hope and despair. She'd only just started to have contractions…

'Diego.' Gus came in and shook his hand.

'How is she?'

'Scared,' Gus said, and gave him a brief rundown of his findings. 'We've given her steroids to mature the baby's lungs and we're trying to stop the labour or at least slow down the process to give the medication time to take effect.'

'Oh, God…' Guilt washed over him, a guilt he knew was senseless, but guilt all the same. However, Gus was one step ahead of him.

'Nothing Izzy or you did contributed to this, Diego. I've spoken with Izzy at length, this was going to happen. In fact…' he gave Diego a grim smile '…an ultrasound and cord study have just been done. Her placenta is small and the cord very thin. This baby really will do better on the outside, though we'd all like to buy another week or two. I knew the baby was small for dates. Izzy was going to have an ultrasound early next week, but from what I've just seen Izzy's baby really will do better by being born.'

'She's been eating well, taking care of herself.'

'She suffered trauma both physically and emotionally early on in the pregnancy,' Gus said. 'Let's just get her through tonight, but guilt isn't going to help anyone.'

Diego knew that. He'd had the same conversation with more parents than he could remember—the endless search for answers, for reasons, when sometimes Mother Nature worked to her own agenda.

'Does she want to see me?'

Gus nodded. 'She doesn't want to call her family just yet.'

When he saw her, Diego remembered the day he had first met her when she had come to the neonatal ward. Wary, guarded, she sat on the bed, looking almost angry, but he knew she was just scared.

'It's going to be okay,' Diego said, and took her hand, but she pulled it away.

'You don't know that.'

She sat there and she had all her make-up on, her hair immaculate, except she was in a hospital gown with a drip and a monitor strapped to her stomach, and Diego wondered if she did actually want him there at all.

She did.

But how could she ask him to be there for her?

She was scared for her baby, yet she resented it almost.

Nine weeks.

They'd had nine weeks left of being just a couple, which was not long by anyone's standards. Nine weeks to get to know each other properly, to enjoy each other, and now even that nine weeks was being denied to them.

How could she admit how much she wanted him to stay—yet how could she land all this on him?

'I think you should go.'

'Izzy.' Diego kept his voice steady. 'Whatever helps you now is fine by me. I can call your family. I can stay with you, or I can wait outside, or if you would prefer that I leave...'

He wanted to leave, Izzy decided, or he wouldn't have said it. The medication they had given her to slow down the labour made her brain work slower, made her thought process muddy.

'I don't know...' Her teeth were chattering, her admission honest. Gus was back, talking to a midwife and Richard Brooke, the paediatric consultant, who had just entered the room. They were all looking at the printout from the monitor and Izzy wanted five minutes alone with Diego, five minutes to try and work out whether or not he wanted to be there, but she wasn't going to get five minutes with her thoughts for a long while.

'Izzy.' She knew that voice and so did Diego, knew that brusque, professional note so well, because they had both used it themselves when they bore bad tidings. 'The baby is struggling; its heartbeat is irregular...'

'It needs time to let the medication take effect.' Izzy's fuzzy logic didn't work on Gus. He just stood over her, next to Diego, both in suits and looking sombre, and she felt as if she were lying in a coffin. 'We want to do a Caesarean, your baby needs to be born.'

Already the room was filling with more staff. She felt the jerk as the brakes were kicked off the bed, the clang as portable oxygen was lifted onto the bed and even in her drugged state she knew this wasn't your standard Caesarean section, this was an emergency Caesarean.

'Is there time...?' She didn't even bother to finish her sentence. Izzy could hear the deceleration in her baby's heartbeat, and knew there wouldn't be time for an epidural, that she would require a general anaesthetic, and it was the scariest, out-of-control feeling. 'Can you be there, Diego?' Her eyes swung from Diego to Gus. 'Can Diego be in there?'

For a general anaesthetic, partners or relatives weren't allowed to come into the theatre, but the NICU team were regularly in Theatre and after just the briefest pause Richard agreed, but with clarification. 'Just for Izzy.'

'Sure,' Diego agreed, and at that moment he'd have agreed to anything, because the thought of being sent to another waiting room, *knowing* all that could go wrong, was unbearable, but as he helped speed the bed the short distance to Theatre, Diego also knew that if there was a problem with the babe, he wanted to be the one dealing with it. This was no time for arrogance neither was it time for feigned modesty—quite simply Diego knew he was the best.

The theatre sister gave Diego a slightly wide-eyed look as she registered he was holding hands with her emergency admission, whom she recognised too.

'Diego's here with Izzy,' the midwife explained. 'Richard has okayed him to go in.'

'Then you'll need to go and get changed,' came the practical response. 'You can say goodbye to her here.'

And that was it.

Diego knew when he saw her again, she would be under anaesthetic.

Izzy knew it too.

'I'm glad you're here...' She was trying not to cry and her face was smothered with the oxygen mask. 'You'll make sure...'

'Everything is going to be fine.' His voice came out

gruffer than he was used to hearing it. He was trying to reassure her, but Diego felt it sounded as if he was telling her off. 'Better than fine,' he said again. His voice still didn't soften, but there wasn't time to correct it. 'Thirty-one-weekers do well.'

'Thirty-two's better.'

'I'll be there,' Diego said. 'And it *is* going to be okay.'

He couldn't give her a kiss, because they were already moving her away.

He turned to Gus, who as her GP would also have to wait outside the operating theatre, and exchanged a look with the worried man. 'Go and get changed, Diego,' Gus said, and his words shocked Diego into action. He changed his clothes in a moment, then put on a hat and made his way through to Theatre.

'Diego!' Hugh, the paediatric anaesthetist greeted him from behind a yellow mask. 'Extremely bradycardic, ready for full resus.'

'Diego's here with the mother.' Brianna was there too, ready to receive the baby, and her unusually pointed tone was clearly telling her colleague to shut the hell up.

The surgeon on duty that night had already started the incision, and Diego knew the man in question was brilliant at getting a baby out urgently when required, but for Diego the world was in slow motion, the theatre clock hand surely sticking as it moved past each second marker.

'Breech.' The surgeon was calling for more traction. Diego could see the two spindly legs the surgeon held in one hand and for the first time in Theatre he felt nausea, understood now why relatives were kept out and almost wished he had been, because suddenly he appreciated how fathers-to-be must feel.

Except he wasn't the father, Diego told himself as the baby's limp body was manoeuvred out and the head delivered.

This baby wasn't his to love, Diego reminded himself as an extremely floppy baby was dashed across to the resuscitation cot.

He *never* wanted to feel like this again.

He never wanted to stand so helpless, just an observer. It would, for Diego, have been easier to work on her himself, yet he was in no state to.

He could feel his fingertips press into her palms with impatience as Hugh called twice for a drug, and though the team was fantastic, their calm professionalism riled him. Richard was fantastic, but Diego would have preferred Megan. Megan pounced on tiny details faster than anyone Diego had seen.

'She's still bradycardic,' Diego said, when surely they should have commenced massage now.

'Out.' Brianna mouthed the word and jerked her head to the theatre doors, but he hesitated.

'Diego!' Brianna said his name, and Diego stiffened in realisation—this wasn't his call, only it felt like it.

Brianna's brown eyes lifted again to his when Diego would have preferred them to stay on the baby, and he knew he was getting in the way, acting more like a father than a professional, so he left before he was formally asked to.

CHAPTER TEN

'THAT'S it, Izzy...' She could hear a male voice she didn't recognise. 'Stay on your back.'

She was under blankets and wanted to roll onto her side, except she couldn't seem to move.

'You're doing fine,' came the unfamiliar voice. 'Stay nice and still.'

'Izzy, it's all okay.'

There was a voice she knew. Strong and deep and accented, and she knew it was Diego, she just didn't know why, and then she opened her eyes and saw his and she remembered.

'You've got a daughter.' His face was inches away. 'She's okay, she's being looked after.'

And then it was fog, followed by pain, followed by drugs, so many drugs she struggled to focus when Diego came back in the afternoon with pictures of her baby.

'She looks like you,' Diego said, but all Izzy could see were tubes.

'Are you working today?'

Diego shook his head. 'No. I just came in to see you.' And he sat down in the chair by her bed and Izzy went to sleep. He flicked through the photos and tried very hard to only see tubes, because this felt uncomfortably familiar, this felt a little like it had with Fernando and he just couldn't go there again.

He certainly wasn't ready to go there again.

There was a very good reason that a normal pregnancy lasted forty weeks, Diego reflected, putting the photos on her locker and heading for home—and it wasn't just for the baby. The parents needed every week of that time to prepare themselves emotionally for the change to their lives.

He wasn't even a parent.

It was Tuesday night and a vicious UTI later before anything resembling normal thought process occurred and a midwife helped her into a chair and along with her mother wheeled her down to the NICU, where, of course, any new mum would want to be if her baby was.

'We take mums down at night all the time,' the midwife explained, when Izzy said the next day would be fine. 'It's no problem.'

Except, privately, frankly, Izzy would have preferred to sleep.

Izzy knew she was a likely candidate for postnatal depression.

As a doctor she was well versed in the subject and the midwives had also gently warned her and given her leaflets to read. Gus too had talked to her—about her difficult labour, the fact she had been separated from her daughter and her difficult past. He'd told her he was there if she needed to talk and he had been open and upfront and told her not to hesitate to reach out sooner rather than later, as had Jess.

She sat in a wheelchair at the entrance to NICU, at the very spot where she had first flirted with Diego, where the first thawing of her heart had taken place, and it seemed a lifetime ago, not a few short weeks.

And, just as she had felt that day, Izzy was tempted to ask the midwife to turn the chair around, more nervous at meeting her baby than she could ever let on. Diego was on a stint of night duty and she was nervous of him seeing her in her new role too, because his knowing eyes wouldn't miss anything. What if she couldn't summon whatever feelings and emotions it was that new mums summoned?

'I bet you can't wait!' Izzy's mum said as the midwife pressed the intercom and informed the voice on the end of their arrival. Then the doors buzzed and she was let in. Diego came straight over and gave her a very nice smile and they made some introductions. 'Perhaps you could show Izzy's mother the coffee room.' Diego was firm on this as he would be with any of his mothers. If Izzy had stepped in and said she'd prefer her mum to come, then of course it would have happened, but Izzy stayed quiet, very glad of a chance to meet her daughter alone.

'I already know where the coffee room is,' Gwen said, 'and I've already seen the baby.'

'Izzy hasn't.' Diego was straight down the line. 'We can't re-create the delivery room but we try—she needs time alone to greet her baby.'

Which told her.

'You know the rules.' He treated Izzy professionally and she was very glad of it. They went through the hand-washing ritual and he spoke to her as they did so.

'Brianna is looking after her tonight,' Diego said. 'Do you know her?'

'I don't think so.'

'She's great—she was there at the delivery. I'll take you over.'

Nicola, Toby's mother, was there and gave Izzy a sympathetic smile as she was wheeled past, which Izzy returned too late, because she was already there at her baby's cot.

Brianna greeted her, but Izzy was hardly listening. Instead she stared into the cot and there she was—her baby. And months of fear and wondering all hushed for a moment as she saw her, her little red scrunched-up face and huge dark blue eyes that stared right into Izzy's.

Over the last three days Diego had bought her plenty of photos, told her how well she was doing and how beautiful she was, but seeing her in the flesh she was better than beautiful, she was hers.

'We're just giving her a little oxygen,' Brianna explained as Diego was called away. 'Which we will be for a couple more weeks, I'd expect...' She opened the porthole and Izzy needed no invitation. She held her daughter's hand, marvelling that such a tiny hand instinctively curled around her index finger, and Izzy knew there and then that she was in love.

'She looks better than I thought...' Izzy couldn't actually believe just how well she looked. Her mum had been crying when she'd returned the first day from visiting her granddaughter and Richard, the consultant paediatrician, had told her that her baby had got off to a rocky start.

'She struggled for the first forty-eight hours, which we were expecting,' Brianna said calmly, 'but she picked up well.'

Diego had said the same, but she'd been worried he'd just been reassuring her, but now she was here, now she could see her, all Izzy could feel was relief and this overwhelming surge charging through her veins that she figured felt a lot like love.

'Now, would you like to hold her?' Brianna said to Izzy's surprise. 'She's due for a feed, but she needs it soon, so would you like to give her a cuddle first?'

She very much would.

Brianna brought over a large chair and Izzy sat, exhausted, then got a new surge of energy.

'Open up your pyjama top,' Brianna said

'It's popping open all the time...' Izzy said, staring down at her newly massive breasts that strained the buttons.

'Your skin will keep her warm and it's good for both of you.'

She hadn't expected so much so soon. Her dreams had been filled with tiny floppy babies like ugly skinned rabbits, yet her baby was prettier and healthier than her photos had shown. Brianna was calm and confident and then there she was, wearing just a nappy and hat and resting on her chest, a blanket being wrapped around them both, skin on skin, and Izzy at that moment knew...

She knew, as far as anyone could possibly know, that the doom and gloom and the shadow of PND was not going to darken her door.

She could feel her baby on her skin and it was almost, Izzy was sure, as if all the darkness just fell away from her now, as pure love flooded in.

A white, pure love that was tangible, that was real. All the fears, the doubts, the dark, dark dread faded, because she had never been sure, really, truly sure that love *could* win, that love would come, that it would happen.

But it just did.

Diego witnessed it too.

He had seen many moments like this one, both in NICU and in the delivery room, and it was more something he ticked off his list than felt moved by—especially in NICU, where bonding was more difficult to achieve. Only it wasn't a list with Izzy, because it did move him, so much so that he came over and smiled down as he watched.

It crossed so many lines, because he didn't want to feel it, and also, as Gwen came over, Diego realised he had sent her own mother away.

Yet he was here.

'She's a Ross all over, isn't she?' Gwen said, and Diego saw Izzy's jaw clench as her mother stamped her territory on her granddaughter and told her how it would be. 'There's nothing of him in her.'

Of course, Henry's parents begged to differ when they came two days later to visit.

They had been in France, trying to have a break, after the most traumatic of months, and had cut their holiday short to come in and visit what was left of their son.

It was an agonising visit. Emotions frayed, Henry's mother teary, his father trying to control things, telling Izzy their rights, blaming her at every turn till she could see clearly where Henry got it from! And, that evening, as soon as they left, Izzy sat on the bed with her fingers pressed into her eyes, trying to hold it together, wondering if now tears would come.

'Bad timing?' Izzy jumped as heard footsteps and saw Josh, the new consultant, at her door. 'I'll come by another time.'

'I'm fine.' Izzy forced a smile. 'Come in.'

'You're sure?' he checked, and Izzy nodded.

'I'm sorry to mess up the roster.'

'That's the last thing you should be worrying about,' Josh replied, just as any boss would in the circumstances, and it was going to be an awkward visit, Izzy knew that. A guy like Josh didn't really belong in the maternity ward with teary women. 'Ben's on leave, but he rang and told me you'd be stressing about details like that, and could I come up and tell you that you're not to worry about a thing and that if there's anything we can do for you, you're to ask.

'Is there anything,' Josh pushed, 'that we can do for you now?'

'I'm being very well looked after. I'm fine, really, it's just been a difficult evening.' She waited for a thin line from Josh about the baby blues, or something like that, but he just looked at her for a long time before he spoke.

'I'm quite sure this is all very difficult for you,' Josh said.

And he was just so disarmingly nice that Izzy found herself admitting a little more. 'Henry's parents just stopped by. They've gone to see the baby.'

'Henry's your late husband?' Josh checked, and Izzy nodded.

'I'm sure you've heard all the gossip.'

'I don't listen to gossip,' Josh said, 'though Ben did bring me up to date on what happened before you came back to work, just so that I would know to look out for you. You know Ben's not into gossip either, but he felt I should know—not all of it, I'm sure, but he told me enough that I can see you'd be having a tough time of it.'

His directness surprised her. Instead of sitting stiffly in the chair and making painful small talk, he came over and sat on the bed, took her hand and gave it a squeeze and a bit of that Irish charm, and Izzy could see why he was such a wonderful doctor.

'Henry's parents blame me,' Izzy admitted. 'They thought our marriage was perfect, they think I'm making it all up.'

'They probably want to believe that you're making it all up,' Josh said wisely.

'They were in tears just before, saying what a wonderful father Henry would have been, how a baby would have changed things, would have saved our marriage, if only I hadn't asked him to leave. They don't know what went on behind closed doors.'

'They need to believe that you're lying,' Josh said. 'But you know the truth.'

'A baby wouldn't have changed things.' With his gentle guidance Izzy's voice was finally adamant. 'Babies don't fix a damaged marriage. That was why I had to leave. I can't even begin to imagine us together as parents. A baby should come from love…'

'Do you want me to call Diego for you?' Josh said, but Izzy shook her head.

'He's already been to visit,' Izzy said. 'He's on a night shift tonight. I can't ring him for every little thing.'

'Yes,' a voice said from the doorway, 'you can.' There stood Diego, but only for a moment, and she dropped Josh's hand as he walked over.

'I'll leave you to it.' Josh smiled and stood up. 'Now, remember, if there's anything we can do, you just pick up that phone. Even if it's just a decent coffee, you've got a whole team behind you twenty-four seven. Just let us know.'

Izzy thanked him, but she sat there blushing as he left and waited till the door was closed.

'Nothing was happening.' Izzy was awash with guilt. 'I was just upset, so he held my hand—'

'Izzy!' Diego interrupted. 'I'm glad Josh was here, I'm glad you had someone to hold your hand.'

Yet she still felt more explanation was needed. 'Henry would have had a fit if he'd—'

'Izzy! I'm not Henry—I don't care how many times I have to say it—I'm nothing like him.'

And he wasn't.

She leant on his broad chest and heard the regular beat of his heart, felt the safe wall of his chest and the wrap of his arms, and if she didn't love her so, it would be so easy to resent her baby—because nine weeks of just them would have been so very nice.

'I'd better go.' Reluctantly he stood up. 'I'll drop by in the morning and let you know what sort of night she had.'

'Tilia,' Izzy said.

'Tilia,' Diego repeated, and a smile spread over his face. 'I like it. What does it mean?'

'It's actually a tree...' Izzy's eyes never left his face, because somehow his reaction was important. 'I'm only telling you this—my mum would freak and I can't have a proper conversation with Henry's parents. It's a lime tree. Henry proposed under this gorgeous old lime tree...' Still he just looked. 'We were happy then.'

'I think it's wonderful,' Diego said. 'And one day, Izzy, you'll be able to talk about him to Tilia, and tell her about those good times.' He gave her a kiss and headed for work, and Izzy lay back on the pillow and even though he'd said everything right, she still couldn't settle.

She looked at new photos of herself holding Tilia and she didn't see the drips or tubes, she just saw her baby.

And there in one photo was a side view of Diego.

The three of them together, except he wasn't kneeling down with his arms around her.

She couldn't imagine these past weeks without him.

Yet she was too scared to indulge in a glimpse of a future with him.

She kept waiting for the axe to fall—sure, quite sure that something this good could never last.

A midwife took her drip down and turned off the lights but the room was still bright thanks to the full moon bathing St Piran's, and while Izzy couldn't get to sleep, Diego on the other hand would have loved to because between visiting Izzy and working he still hadn't caught up from Tilia's rapid arrival.

It was a busy night that kept him at the nurses' station rather than the shop floor, where Diego preferred to be.

And, worse, from the computer he could hear her crying.

He glanced up and Brianna was checking a drug with another nurse working at the next cot, and Diego could hear Tilia crying. Brianna must have asked the other nurse for an opinion on something, because they were reading through the obs sheet. It was *normal* for babies to cry—he barely even heard it, so why did he stand up and head over?

'Brianna.' He jerked his head to Tilia's cot and he wished he hadn't, knew he was doing something he never would have done previously. If a baby was crying it was breathing was the mantra when matters where pressing. But Brianna didn't seem worried at his snap. Actually, she was more discreet than anyone he had ever met, but he could have sworn he saw her lips suppress a smile.

And as for Josh, well, as tired as he might be, bed was the last thing he wanted.

He'd visited Izzy when really he hadn't had to. Ben had actually asked for him to drop in over the next couple of days, but Josh had convinced himself that it was his duty to go after his shift.

Then, having visited her, he had hung around till someone had made some joke about him not having a home to go to, so eventually he'd headed there, but had stopped at the garage first.

As he pulled up at the smart gated community and the gates opened, Josh checked his pager and knew in his heart of hearts he was hoping against hope for something urgent to call him in.

God, had it really come to this, sitting in his driveway, steeling himself to go inside?

Izzy's words rang in his ears.

'A baby wouldn't have changed things… Babies don't fix a damaged marriage… I can't even begin to imagine us together as parents… A baby should come from love…'

There *had* been love between him and Rebecca.

A different sort of love, though, not the intense, dangerous love he had once briefly known. That had been a love so consuming that it had bulldozed everything in its path. He closed his eyes and leant back on the headrest and for the first time in years he fully let himself visit that time.

Felt the grief and the agony, but it was too painful to recall so instead he dwelt on the consequences of raw love—a love that ruined lives and could destroy plans, a love that had threatened his rapid ascent in his career.

His and Rebecca's love had been different—safer certainly.

She wanted a successful doctor—*that* he could provide.

They had been good for each other, had wanted the same, at least for a while.

Josh could see her shadow behind the blinds, see her earrings, her jewellery, the skimpy outlines of her nightdress that left nothing to the imagination, and knew what Rebecca wanted from him tonight.

And he also knew that it wasn't about him.

'At least I'll have something to show for four years of marriage…' He recalled the harsh words of their latest row and then watched as she poured herself a drink from the decanter. He felt a stab of sympathy as he realised that Rebecca needed a bit of Dutch courage to go through with tonight.

Maybe he should get a vasectomy without her knowing, but what sort of coward, or husband, did that? Josh reeled at his own thought.

So he checked his pocket for his purchase from the garage, because he couldn't face her tears from another rejection. They hadn't slept together in weeks, not since…

Josh slammed that door in his mind closed, simply refused to go there, and tried very hard not to cloud the issue. In truth his and Rebecca's marriage had been well into injury time long before they had come to St Piran.

He went to pocket the condoms, to have them conveniently to hand, because no doubt Rebecca would ensure they never made it up the stairs and he knew for a fact she'd stopped taking the Pill.

'What the hell am I doing?' he groaned.

Yes, it would be so much easier to go in and make love.

Easier in the short term perhaps to give her the baby Rebecca said she wanted.

But since when had Josh chosen the easy path?

He tossed the condoms back into the glove box, a guarantee of sorts that he wouldn't give in and take the easy way out.

There was a conversation that needed to take place and, no matter how painful, it really was time.

They owed each other that at least.

Taking a breath, he walked up the neat path of his low-maintenance garden, waved to his neighbours, who were sipping wine on their little balcony and watching the world go by.

'Beautiful night, Josh.'

'It's grand, isn't it?' Josh agreed, and turned the key and stepped inside.

To the world, to his neighbours, the dashing doctor was coming home after a hellishly long day to his wonderful smart home and into the loving arms of his beautiful trophy wife.

It *was* a beautiful night.

The moon was big and round and it just accentuated the chaos as Evelyn Harris surveyed the ruin of her kitchen, plates smashed and broken, her ribs bruised and tender, the taste of blood in her mouth. She heard her husband snoring upstairs in bed.

She picked up the phone and not for the first time wondered about calling Izzy—but would the doctor even remember her? Surely it was too late to ring at this hour, and her son had an exam in the morning and she had lunch with John's boss's wife to get through, so she put down the phone and chose to sleep on the plush leather sofa.

Izzy was right.

Nobody *did* know what went on behind closed doors.

CHAPTER ELEVEN

'SHE'S a tough little one.'

Like her mother, Diego thought.

Tilia, though small for dates and premature, was also incredibly active and strong. She had only required a short time on CPAP and was doing well on oxygen.

It really was a case of better out than in—now she could gain weight and as was often the case with babies who had been deprived nutrition *in utero*, Tilia's forehead often creased in concern as if she was constantly worried as to where her next meal was coming from.

'She wants her mum.' Brianna could not get Tilia to settle. 'I might ring Maternity and see if Izzy's still awake, she might get a nice cuddle. Then I'm going to have my coffee break. Could you watch mine for a moment while I call?'

They often rang Maternity, especially when babies were active and if there was a nurse who could bring the mother over—well, the middle of the night was a nice time to sit in rocking chair and bond a little. But when Diego had left Izzy she had been drained and exhausted and she could really use a full night's sleep—not that he was going to say that to Brianna. The gossip was already flying around the hospital since their appearance at the ball—had a certain little lady not put in such an early appearance, they might have been old news now, but given the turn of events and that Diego had been in the labour ward and was up twice day visiting on Maternity, he felt as if all eyes were on them. The scrutiny was just too fierce and strong at such a fragile time.

He was actually more than glad to be on nights, away from Rita's probing, and he had deliberately allocated Brianna to care for Tilia.

Brianna was one of the most private people Diego had met. She said nothing about her private life. She was there to work and work she did, loving and caring for her charges—gossip the last thing she was interested in.

'They've given Izzy a sleeping tablet,' Brianna said when she came back. 'Never mind, little lady, I'll give you a cuddle.'

'You go and have your break,' Diego said. 'I'll sort her.'

He didn't want to be doing this.

Or had he engineered it?

Diego didn't want to examine his feelings. Brianna was long overdue her coffee break, it was as simple as that. So he washed his hands in his usual thorough manner, put on a gown and then unclipped the sides of the incubator.

Often, so very often he did this—soothed a restless baby, or took over care while one of his team took their break.

And tonight it would be far safer to remember that.

He would sit and get this baby settled and perhaps chat with another nurse as he did so, or watch the ward from a chair.

He sat and expertly held Tilia, spoke as he always did to his charges—joking that he would teach her a little Spanish.

Which he did.

Then Chris, another of the nurses on duty that night, came over and asked him to run his eyes over a drug.

Which he did.

And then he felt something he hadn't in more than a decade.

Something he had tried never to feel since Fernando.

He adored his babies, but they weren't *his* to love.

He had loved Fernando, had held him three times in his little life, and it had never come close since.

But holding Tilia, it came close.

Dangerously close.

She wasn't a patient and she wasn't his new girl-friend's baby.

She was Tilia.

Izzy's baby.

But more than that.

He smelt that unmistakable baby smell that surrounded him each day but which he never noticed, he looked into huge eyes that were the same shape as her mother's and she had the same shape mouth. Even her nostrils were the same.

And there, sitting with all the hissing and bleeping

and noise that was a busy neonatal unit, Diego, felt a stab of dread.

That he might lose her too.

He looked over to where Toby's mother had come in, restless and unable to sleep, for just one more check on her son, and he knew how she felt—how many times in the night at eighteen he had woken with a sudden shock of fright and rushed to check on Fernando, asking the nurses to check and check again, petrified that they had missed something, but it wasn't that fear that gripped him as he held Tilia.

'You're going to be fine,' Diego said to Tilia in Spanish. 'You're going to be clever and grow healthy and strong...'

Only would he be around to see it?

'And your mother's getting stronger each day too,' Diego went on. 'Just watch her grow too.'

He wanted that for Izzy. He vowed as he sat there, holding her baby while she could not, that he would help Izzy grow, would do everything to encourage her, even if that meant that she grew away from him.

How could he let himself fall in love with this little babe when who knew what her mother might want days, weeks or months from now? When who knew what he might want?

Diego ran a finger down her little cheek.

But how could he not?

Staying in the parents' wing had been the right choice.

It was a precious time, one where she caught up on

all she had missed out on, one where there was nothing to focus on other than her baby.

Always Diego was friendly, professional, calm, except for the visits before or after her shift, when he was friendly and calm but he dropped the professional for tender, but there was never any pressure, no demands for her time. Now, as Tilia hit four weeks, the world outside was starting to creep back in and for the first time since her daughter's birth, Izzy truly assessed the situation, wondering, fearing that it was as she had suspected—that her daughter's birth had changed everything for them, that his lack of demands meant a lack of passion.

A soft rap at her door at six-thirty a.m. didn't wake her. She'd been up and fed Tilia and had had her shower, and often Diego popped in at this time if he was on an early shift, bearing two cups of decent coffee and, this morning, two croissants.

'She went the whole night without oxygen.' Izzy beamed.

'We'll be asking her to leave if she carries on like this!' Diego joked, and though Izzy smiled and they chatted easily, when he left a familiar flutter took place in her stomach. Tilia was doing well, really well, and though at first the doctors had warned it could be several weeks before her discharge, just four short weeks on Tilia was defying everyone—putting on weight, managing the occasional bottle, and now a whole night without oxygen and no de-sats. Discharge day would be coming soon, Izzy knew, but if Tilia was ready, Izzy wasn't so sure she was.

Diego was working the floor today. Once a week he left his office and insisted on doing the job he adored. From nine a.m. he was working in Theatre with a multiple birth and a baby with a cardiac defect scheduled for delivery. The unit was expecting a lot of new arrivals, and it fell to him to tell the mother of a thriving thirty-five-weeker that her room would be needed in a couple of days.

He'd stretched it to the limit, of course.

Not just because it was Izzy, not just that she was a doctor at this hospital, but with all she had been through, he would have done his best for any woman in that situation—though he waited till he was working to tell her.

'She won't take it.' Izzy was in the nursery, feeding her daughter, jiggling the teat in Tilia's slack mouth. 'She took the last one really well...'

He tickled her little feet and held his hand over Izzy's and pushed the teat in a bit more firmly, tried to stimulate the baby to suck, but Tilia was having none of it, her little eyelids flickering as she drifted deeper into sleep. Izzy actually laughed as she gave in.

'She's not going to take it.' There was no panic in her voice, Diego noted. Izzy was a pretty amazing mum. Often with doctors or nurses they were more anxious than most new parents and even though he'd expected that from Izzy, she'd surprised him. She revelled in her new motherhood role and was far more relaxed than most.

'They're like teenagers,' Diego said, 'party all night, and sleep all day. That last feed would have exhausted her.'

Chris, one of the nurses, came over and saw the full

bottle, and because Tilia was so small and needed her calories, she suggested they tube-feed her, and Izzy went to stand to help.

'Actually, Chris, I need a word with Izzy.'

'Sure.' Chris took Tilia and Izzy sat, frowning just a little, worried what was to come because Diego, when at work, never brought his problems to the shop floor.

'Is she okay?' Her first thought was something had been said on the ward round that morning and he was about to give her bad news.

'She's wonderful,' Diego assured her. 'So wonderful, in fact, that I need your room for some parents we are getting whose baby will not be doing so well.'

'Oh.'

'I know it seems pretty empty over in the parents' wing at the moment, but I'm getting some transfers from other hospitals today, and I have some mothers in Maternity now needing accommodation too. You don't need to leave today...'

'But it would help?'

'It would,' Diego admitted. Normally they gave more notice, but Izzy had been told last week that if the room was needed, given her close proximity to the hospital and Tilia's improving status, she was top of the list to leave if required. Izzy had been happy with that. Well, till the inevitable happened.

How could she tell Diego that she didn't want to go home?

More than that, she had never wanted to bring her baby back to the home she had shared with Henry.

'Izzy!' Rita was at the nursery door. 'You've got visitors. Mr and Mrs Bailey, Tilia's grandparents...'

He saw her lips tense and then stretch out into a smile and he'd have given anything not to be on duty now, to just be here with her as she faced all this, but Diego knew it would surly only make things worse. So instead he stood, smiled as he would at any other relatives and said to Izzy, 'I'll leave you to it.' Just as he would to any of the mums—except he knew so much more.

'Could I have a word, Doctor?' Mr. Bailey followed him out.

'I'm not a doctor; I'm the nurse unit manager. Is there anything I can help you with?'

Up shot the eyebrows, just as Diego expected. 'I'd prefer to speak to a doctor,' Mr Bailey said. 'You see, we're not getting enough information from Izzy. She just says that Tilia is doing well and as her grandparents we have a right to know more.'

'Tilia *is* doing well,' Diego said. 'We're very pleased with her progress.'

'I'm not sure if you're aware of the circumstances. Our beloved son passed away and Izzy is doing her level best to keep us out of the picture. Tilia's extremely precious to us and we will not be shut out.'

And at that moment all Diego felt was tired for Izzy.

'I'd really prefer to speak with a doctor.'

Which suited Diego fine. 'I'll just check with Izzy and then I can page—'

'Why would you check with her? I've already told you that she's doing her level best to keep us misinformed. I know she seems quite pleasant, but she's a manipulative—'

'Mr Bailey.' Diego halted him—oh, there were many things, so many things he would have loved to have said, but he was far better than that. 'I will first speak to Tilia's mother. Let's see what she says and then we can take it from there.'

Of course she said yes.

Diego looked over when Richard agreed to speak to them and could see Izzy sitting by Tilia, looking bemused and bewildered, and if he'd done his level best to keep work and his private life separate, right now he didn't care.

'They don't trust me to tell them everything!' Izzy blew her fringe upwards. 'They're annoyed I waited two days to ring them after she was born…'

'They're just scared you'll keep them from seeing her.'

'Well, they're going the right way about it!' Izzy shot back, but Diego shook his head.

'Don't go there, Izzy.'

'I won't!' Izzy said, but she was exasperated. 'They've been in every day, I've dressed her in the outfits they've bought, I text them a photo of her each night. What more do they want?'

'Time,' Diego said. 'And so do we.' He glanced over to make sure no one was in earshot 'Do you want to come to my place tonight?' He saw her swallow. 'I'm closer to the hospital. If it makes the transition easier…'

'Just for tonight,' Izzy said, because she didn't want

to foist herself on him, but she couldn't stand to be alone at the house on her first night away from Tilia.

'Sure.'

He got called away then, and Izzy sat there awash with relief, grateful for the reprieve, until it dawned on her.

She was staying the night with Diego.

How the hell could she have overlooked that?

CHAPTER TWELVE

SHE felt incredibly gauche, knocking at his door that evening. 'Where did you disappear to?' he asked as he let her in. 'I wasn't sure if you were coming.'

'I got a taxi and took my stuff home,' Izzy said airily, because she certainly wasn't going to admit she'd spent the afternoon in the bathroom—trying and failing to whip her postnatal body into suitable shape for Diego's eyes. 'By the time I got back for her evening feed, your shift had ended.'

'You've got hospital colour!' Diego smiled as she stood in the lounge. 'I never noticed it on the ward but now you are here in the real world, I can see it.'

There was a distinct lack of mirrors in Diego's flat, so Izzy would just have to take his word for it, but she was quite sure he was right. Apart from an occasional walk around the hospital grounds, a few very brief trips home and one trip out with Megan, she'd been living under fluorescent lighting and breathing hospital air, and no doubt her skin had that sallow tinge that patients often had when they were discharged after a long stay.

'Have a seat out on the balcony,' Diego suggested. 'Get some sun. I'll join you in a minute.'

It *was* good to sit in the evening sun. Izzy could feel it warming her cheeks and she drank in the delicious view—the moored boats and a few making their way back in. There was no place nicer than St Piran on a rosy summer evening, made nicer when Diego pressed a nice cold glass of champagne in her hand.

'One of the joys of bottle-feeding!' Diego said, because Izzy's milk supply had died out two weeks in.

And then he was back to his kitchen and Izzy could only sit and smile.

He was such a delicious mix.

So male, so sexy, yet there was this side to him that could address, without a hint of a blush or a bat of an eyelid, things that most men knew little about.

'How does it feel to be free?' Diego called from the kitchen as she picked a couple of tomatoes out of the pots that lined his balcony.

'Strange,' Izzy called, but he was already back. 'I keep waiting for my little pager to go off to let me know she needs feeding. I feel guilty, actually.'

'It's good to have a break before you bring her home.'

'Most new mums don't get it.'

'Most new mums have those extra weeks to prepare,' Diego said, arranging some roasted Camembert cheese and breadsticks on the table, which Izzy fell on, scooping up the sticky warm goo with a large piece of bread.

'I've been craving this,' Izzy said. 'How did you know?'

'Tonight, you get everything that has been forbidden to you in pregnancy, well, almost everything. Some things can wait!' Diego said, as Izzy's toes curled in her sandals. His grin was lazy and slow and she hated how he never blushed, hated that her cheeks were surely scarlet. God, she'd forgotten how they sizzled, Izzy thought as he headed back to prepare dinner.

There *were* so many sides to Diego and recently she'd been grateful for the professional side to him and for the care he had shown off duty too, but she was in his territory now, not pregnant, not a patient, not a parent on the unit. Tonight she was just Izzy, whoever Izzy was.

And that night she started to remember.

'You can cook!' Izzy exclaimed as he brought a feast out to her—shellfish, mussels, oysters, prawns and cream cheese wrapped in roast peppers, and all the stuff she'd craved in the last few weeks of her pregnancy.

'Not really. You could train a monkey to cook seafood.' Diego shrugged. 'And the antipasto is from our favourite café...'

She didn't know if it was the champagne or the company, but talking to Diego was always easy so she figured it was the latter. They talked, and as the sky turned to navy they laughed and they talked, and more and more she came back.

Not even Izzy Bailey, but a younger Izzy, an Izzy Ross, who she had stifled and buried and forgotten.

Izzy Ross, who teased and joked and did things like lean back in her seat and put her feet up on his thighs, Izzy Ross, who expected a foot rub and Diego obliged.

But it was Izzy Bailey who was convinced things were all about to change.

'So, what did the real estate agent say?'

'That it's a good offer!' Izzy poked out her tongue. 'It's not, of course, but it's better than the last one, though they want a quick settlement.'

'Which is what you wanted?'

'When I was pregnant and hoping to find somewhere before she was born.' She looked at him. 'In a few days she'll be home,' Izzy said, 'and as well as having a baby home, I'm going to have to pack up a house and find a new one, and I'm going to have to find a babysitter just so we can *date*.' Her voice wobbled. 'We haven't even slept together and we're talking nappies and babysitters...'

He had the audacity to laugh.

'It's not funny, Diego.'

'You're making problems where there are none. Sex is hardly going to be a problem.'

God, he was so relaxed and assured about it, like it was a given it was going to be marvellous.

The icing on the cake.

'Come on.' He stood up.

'Where are we going?'

'The movies and then there's a nice wine bar, they do music till late...'

'I don't want to go to the movies!' Izzy couldn't believe Mr Sensitive could get it so wrong. 'And if you think I've got the energy to be sitting in a wine bar...'

'I thought you wanted us to date!'

'Ha, ha.'

'Izzy, you need time with your baby and that's the priority. I'll slot in, and if it's an issue that we haven't slept together yet, well, we both know it's going to be great.'

'You don't know that.'

'Oh, I do.' Diego grinned. 'I'm looking forward to getting rid of your hang-ups.'

'Can you get rid of them tonight?'

And suddenly he didn't look so assured.

'It's too soon...'

'No,' Izzy said slowly. 'No heavy lifting, no strenuous exercise...'

'Do you want me, Izzy?' He was always direct and now never more so. 'Or do you just want it over?'

'I don't know,' Izzy admitted, and there should have been a big horn to denote she was giving the wrong answer, but she was incapable of dishonesty with him—or rather she didn't want to go down that route, saying the right thing just to keep *him* happy. She wanted the truth with Diego even if it wasn't what he wanted to hear.

'What are you scared of?'

'That I'll disappoint you,' she admitted. 'Because on so many levels I disappointed him.' She snapped her mouth closed. Diego had made it very clear that he didn't compare to Henry, which he didn't, but... She looked over to where he stood, tried to choose words that could explain her insecurities, but there were none that could do them justice. 'Things weren't great in that department,' she settled for, but Diego's frown just deepened.

'I know I was pregnant and so there must have been a relationship...' She swallowed. 'His parents take it as proof that our marriage was healthy, that...' She couldn't explain further and thankfully she didn't have to because Diego spoke.

'It would be nice,' Diego said slowly, 'if babies were only conceived in love...' There was silence that she didn't break as he thought for a moment. 'If there was some sort of...' Again he paused, trying to find the English for a word he hadn't used in his time in the country '*Cósmico*, contraception.' It was Izzy who then frowned and she gave a small smile.

'Cosmic.'

'Cosmic contraception,' Diego continued, 'where no experimenting teenagers, no rape victims, no women in a terrible relationship who just go along with it to keep the peace...' His strange logic soothed some of the jagged parts of her mind. She liked his vision and it made her smile. 'Here's a happy couple,' Diego continued, 'said the sperm to the egg. You know it doesn't work like that.'

'People think...'

'People are stupid, then.' Diego would not let her go there, would not let her care what others thought. 'People choose to be ignorant rather than face unpleasant truths. You know what your marriage was like and you don't have to live it again, explaining details to me, to justify why you're pregnant. But I will say this.' For the first time his voice bordered on angry. 'If he expected a great sex life, if he was disappointed by your lack of enthusiasm in that department after the way he treated you, then he was the most stupid of them all.'

And he was so convincing that she was almost... convinced.

Almost.

But still the cloud of doubt hung over her and Diego could see it.

It had never been his intention to sleep with her tonight.

For her to stay was a hope, but sex—hell, wasn't that supposed to be the last thing on her mind?

Wasn't it too soon?

And he liked straightforward, only this was anything but.

But he looked over to where she sat, not in the least offended that she wanted it over with, another thing to tick off her list as she moved on with her life. And again it wasn't a time for arrogance or feigned modesty. He knew he was good, knew he could make her happy—and wasn't happy part of their deal?

'I'll sleep with you on one condition.'

Why did he always make her smile?

'That you never fake it for me.'

'Or you.'

'Er, Izzy,' he said, and that made her blush and give an embarrassed laugh.

'I mean, don't pretend afterwards that it's okay, just so you don't upset me.'

Diego rolled his eyes, but he was smiling now too. 'The talking doesn't stop when we get to the bedroom. I can do both!'

And he knew then that they could talk about it for ever, but words could only reassure so far. This was so not what he had imagined for tonight. There was something almost clinical about it and yet Diego had so much confidence in her, in them, in all they were going to be, that if this was a hurdle for her, perhaps it was better to jump it.

He pulled her onto his lap, but his kisses weren't working. He could feel her trying, feel her doing her very best to relax, but he wouldn't put her through it. He pulled back his lips, looked into her eyes and feigned a martyred sigh 'Shall we just get this over with?'

She almost wept with relief.

'Please.'

'Ring the hospital.'

Which took away her little excuse to suddenly stop later. Diego was onto her, she realised.

So she rang and, no, Tilia didn't need her to come in.

Oh, God, what was she doing?

She felt as if she was walking into Theatre for surgery as he took her hand and they headed for the bedroom. Izzy half expected him to tell her to get undressed and pop on a gown and that he'd be back in five minutes.

Couldn't it happen more seamlessly?

Couldn't they just have had a kiss on the balcony and somehow ended up naked on his massive bed without the awkward bit in the middle? But that hadn't worked and Izzy realised she would have been faking it because she would know where it would lead, to this, the bit she was dreading, the part that was holding her back from moving on.

God, it was a room built for nothing but a bed. Izzy gulped.

Massive windows, floorboards and one very large, very low bed and not much else, bar a table that doubled as a washing basket.

'Where are your things?' Izzy would rather deal with basics than the bed.

'What things?'

'Alarm clock, books...' Her hands flailed. 'A mirror, a wardrobe...'

'Here's the wardrobe.'

Okay, there it was, hidden in the wall, but apart from that...

'Curtains?' Izzy begged.

'It looks out to the ocean,' Diego said, and to her horror he was stripping off. 'And I don't need an alarm clock—I wake at five.' He was unbuckling his belt, his top already off, stripping off like a professional and chatting about nothing as Izzy stood, champagne in hand, wishing she'd never started this.

'Five?'

'It's hell.' He pushed his denim jeans down past thick thighs as he explained his plight to a distracted audience. 'Even when the clocks change my brain knows and I wake up.'

Oh, God.

He wasn't *erect* erect, but he was erect enough that it was pointing at her—this conversation going on as this thing waggled and danced and she did her best not to look at it, tried to worry about windows and passing ships, but he was completely naked now.

'Are you always this uninhibited?'

'I've been undressing for bed for many years now,' Diego said, and then his voice was serious. 'Let's just start as we mean to go on.'

But would he want to go on afterwards?

'I've changed my mind,' Izzy said, in the hope of delaying the inevitable, so sure was she that when he found out just how hopeless she was, he wouldn't want her or, worse, would feel stuck with her.

'Why don't we just sleep together?' Diego suggested. 'Given it will probably be our one interrupted night for the foreseeable future.'

And though she wanted to turn and flee, he was right, Izzy realised, because as hellish as this was for her, next time there might be more than passing ships to worry about. There might be a baby in the room too!

'I forgot my phone…'

'Your phone?' Izzy said to his departing back, and as he spoke about staff ringing some nights if there was a problem, and he'd rather that… Izzy took the moment to get out of her clothes and under the sheet before he returned.

Just as Diego had expected her to do.

He didn't need his phone, of course.

And he was, in fact, nervous.

Just not for the same reasons as Izzy.

Diego liked sex.

Correction.

Diego *loved* sex.

And he liked relationships too, but short-term ones. There was nothing short term about Izzy.

As he climbed into bed and turned and faced her, it was the sense of responsibility that unnerved him a touch.

Not just the obvious, not just Izzy and her baby, but a self-imposed responsibility towards Izzy, because in every area of her life she was getting it together, managing it herself, but for this part to be right she needed another, and she had trusted herself to him.

'Better?' Diego asked, and, yes, it was.

Much, much better, not because she was in the dark and under a sheet, just better because she was, for the first time, lying next to him and he was so solid and bulky and just him.

'In a few short weeks,' Diego said into the darkness, 'you'll be ripping your clothes off in the middle of the day and we'll be on the kitchen floor!'

'Your confidence is inspiring.'

'Oh, you will!' Diego said. 'Remember the bath?'

How could she forget?

'That just sort of happened.'

Izzy lived on her nerves.

Diego lived on instinct.

Instinct that told him his parents were wrong, that he'd do better by not following their chosen course for him.

Instinct that had told him over and over again that, despite neat numbers on a chart, a baby was struggling.

And instinct was all very well, but it got in the way sometimes.

Like now, when he knew he should be closing his eyes and trying to sleep, to let her come to him, a little problem arose.

Or rather quite a big problem that crept along the side of her thigh, nudging her like a puppy that wanted to be stroked.

'*Perdón!*' Diego said, and he would have moved away but he heard her sort of laugh and he wasn't a saint. She was right there next to him and naked and warm and he'd had to go and remind them both of that bath.

Yes, it was instinct that drove his lips to her neck, the hand that wasn't under her roaming her body a little and then, for Izzy, instinct overrode nerves.

His lips were soft but firm at the same time, kissing her, breathing onto her skin. Diego, a man who had only ever given, now wanting badly, and from his deep murmurs of approval as his hands slid to her breasts it was her that he wanted.

And she wanted a little more of him too.

She turned and faced him, so she could kiss him properly, not the nervous kiss about where this might lead she had endured on the balcony, but a bolder kiss, knowing where this might lead, in the bedroom.

He tasted of him, his tongue cool and lazy and then suddenly insistent and then back to lazy. He drove her wild with his mouth, because her body was at its own bidding now. Her thighs parted a little and captured him as they kissed, he could feel himself hard but smooth between the tender skin of her thighs, and she wanted him higher, her legs parting, only Diego wasn't rushing.

'I know where you were this afternoon...' His hand

was there, exploring where she had shaved. 'Next time I'll do it.' And she felt this bubble of moisture at the very thought as his fingers slipped in and it felt divine.

'Condoms!' Izzy said, common sense prevailing, even if the last thing she wanted was him getting up and heading for the bathroom.

But this was Diego.

He sort of stretched over her and she felt his arm rummage in the dark beneath the bed and come up with the goods.

Oh, God, he was so male, so... She flailed for a word...basic.

It was the only one she could think of and it didn't really suit, but it was the best she could do.

And then he rolled off her and lay on his back and Izzy came up with another word.

Raw.

He didn't slip it on discreetly as he kissed her. No, he lay back and she watched, she actually propped up on her elbow and watched, this shiver inside as he gave himself two slow strokes, two long, slow strokes that had Izzy licking her lips and feeling suddenly contrary. This was something she had wanted over and done with, something she still wanted over and done with, except she was balling her fist not to reach out and touch him.

So she did.

Like warm silk he slid down her palm, the pulse of him beneath her fingers, and she did it again and it felt so nice that she did it again, till his hand closed around hers and halted her.

'Aren't I doing it right?' said her old fears, and for a moment there was no reply.

'Izzy.' He paused again. 'Any more right and we won't need the condom.'

And then she got her seamless kiss, because that was what he did, he rolled over and kissed her, his tongue, his breath filling her mouth and his body over her and then the nudge of him between her legs.

And she was scared, but she wanted him.

Like hating flying and preparing for take-off, wanting just to get there, except there's a slight delay in departure and cabin crew are bringing round drinks and you taste your first Singapore sling.

Oh, my!

He was slow and tender and, yes, she was ready, and it had little to do with nerves that he had to squeeze inside. Izzy screwed her eyes closed, told herself to breathe as her body stretched to greet him, the slow fill of him more than she could accommodate, except slowly she did.

And then she breathed out as he slid out, right to the tip and she braced herself for him to fill her again, which he did.

And then again and each time she had to remember to breathe.

His elbows held most of his weight, his rough chin was on her cheek and his breath tickled at her ear, and suddenly Izzy remembered where she was and it wasn't happening so easily. She knew she should be a touch more enthusiastic, but she was a mother now and surely sensible, so she made the right noises and lifted her hips and would have settled for his pleasure, except Diego had other ideas.

He smothered her feigned gasps with his mouth and offered her more weight, wrapping his arms around her, kissing her, not harder but deeper, and she remembered his demand that she not fake it. So she lay there and let herself just feel him—lay there as he kissed her eyes and then her cheeks and then she felt the shift in him, the kissing stopping, his heavier weight and the ragged breathing in her ear, and she forgot where she was again, forgot about rather a lot of things, just the delicious feel of him, and the scratch of his jaw and the stirrings of the orgasm he had given her before. Then she found that she *was* making noises now, but of her body's own accord, and as he bucked deep inside her, she did something she would never have envisaged from this night.

'Not yet.'

She was too deep into herself to wonder at the transition to voicing her wants, her real wants, but Diego recognised it and it gave a surge of pleasure that almost tipped him over. He would have waited for this for ever, yet now was struggling to wait another minute, but for Izzy he did.

He could feel her pleasure and it was his.

Both locked in a dance that moved faster than them.

'Not yet!' She was in another place and he could hear her calling and he chased her, he was holding back and driving harder, he could hear her moans, feel the surge in her that was akin to panic, but he knew her body too, could feel her body tight around him, feel her trip and he just knew.

Knew she needed all of him before she could give that bit more.

Her words were futile, Izzy realised, because Diego was moving at a different speed now, reaching for the finish line with a surge of energy that had her breathless.

She could hear her name, feel the unbridled passion and just the sheer strength of him as he thrust inside her. And she stopped trying then, stopped trying to chase or catch him, she just felt the moment.

Felt him over her, in her and his arms behind her, she could hear her name, taste his skin, and then it was his name she heard her voice calling, his name said in a tone she didn't recognise, then a shout of surprise as she let go.

Her thighs were shaking and her hips pushing up against his, her hands digging into his back, and deep inside she trembled as Diego pulsed into her.

And most delicious of all, it didn't matter that she was a teeny bit late for the party, she was there, she had made it, her late entrance dazzling, because he got to feel every beat of it as he delivered those last emptying strokes and instinct had served him well.

As he felt her crash and burn beneath him, as he tried to get his head out of white light and back to the dark, he knew he had just met the real Izzy.

'Tell me again,' Diego said, when he could get the words out, 'what exactly your hang-ups are.'

CHAPTER THIRTEEN

'SHE's fine!' a night nurse greeted her as Izzy dashed in at seven a.m.

She'd given Diego a fifteen-minute head start so they didn't arrive together and it seemed to take ages for the intercom to answer when she buzzed, because the staff were all in handover.

Izzy felt guilty with pleasure and was sure there must be a penance to pay for having such a wonderful night, except Tilia was fine—completely adorable and wide awake. Chris, her nurse for the day, informed Izzy when she came out of handover that Tilia might even be ready for her first bath.

Izzy was glad to have Chris beside her, encouraging her.

Tilia seemed so small and slippery and she wouldn't stop crying.

'I thought they liked their bath,' Izzy said.

'Just rock her a little.'

Which Izzy did, and Tilia's cries softened.

Her tufts of hair were shampooed and by the time Izzy had dried and dressed her, it was all sticking up and Izzy thought her heart would burst as she sat in the rocking chair and held her.

'How soon do you think?' Izzy asked the perpetual question.

'When she's taking all her feeds and just a bit bigger,' Chris said. 'She's doing so well. I know you're impatient to get her home, but she still needs top-ups and a little one like this...' She took an exhausted Tilia from Izzy and popped her in her cot then put the saturation probe on her, checked her obs and popped a little hat on. 'Even a bath wears them out. Why don't you go down to the canteen and get some breakfast?' Chris suggested, rightly guessing that Izzy hadn't eaten.

'Good idea,' Izzy agreed. 'I'll go and see if Nicola wants to come down with me.'

'Actually,' Chris said gently, 'maybe it's best if you leave Nicola for now.'

'Oh!' Izzy waited for more information, only she wasn't a doctor on duty here and there was no information forthcoming. 'I'll be at the canteen, then,' Izzy said. 'I've got my pager.'

She walked through the unit, her eyes drawn to Toby's cot. There was Nicola and her husband, and Diego was sitting with them. His face was more serious than she had ever seen it and Izzy felt sick as Megan came into the unit and instead of waving to Izzy just gave a very brief nod and headed over to them.

It was the longest morning.

Tilia awoke at eleven but wouldn't take her bottle and Izzy came close to crying, except she shook her head when Chris passed her a box of tissues.

'You are allowed to cry.'

But it seemed so petty. Tilia was thriving, okay, a little slower than Izzy would like, but she was getting bigger and stronger every day and, anyway, Izzy knew, there was a lot more to cry over than that—and now just wasn't the time to.

'Hey, where's Chris?' Diego gave her a tired smile as he came in later to get an update.

'Two minutes,' Chris called from the sinks, where she was helping another mum with a bath.

'How are you?' Diego asked.

'Good.'

'Tilia?'

'Misbehaving—she won't take her feeds.'

'She had a bath, though,' Diego said, but she could tell he was distracted and who could blame him?

'How's Toby?'

'He's not good,' Diego said. 'I know you helped deliver him.' He was walking a fine line. 'We can talk another time.'

'Sure.'

'Two more minutes!' Chris called again.

'I'm going to be working late tonight.' His voice was low. 'I can give you a key if you want…'

'I might go home tonight,' Izzy said, hoping he wouldn't take up her offer of an out. 'I'm really tired and you're working…'

Except he took it. 'Sure.'

And then Chris was walking over, ready to bring Diego up to date with her charges, and Izzy didn't see him again apart from the back of his shoulders for the rest of the day.

And that night, when she sat at home, she told herself she was being ridiculous—he was working late, he had every reason to be sombre, and she had been the one to say she'd prefer to go home, but, just as a mother could often pin-point the moment their child became sick long before the doctors were concerned even when the child itself said it was well, Izzy could sense change.

Even as she tried to leave the past where it belonged, she could sense a shift, could sense a black cloud forming, and it had hovered over Diego today.

'Neonatal Unit—Diego speaking.'

'It's me.' Izzy hadn't really expected him to answer the phone. It was edging towards ten p.m., which meant he had done a double shift. 'I was just ringing to check up on Tilia.'

'She's had a good night so far, I think,' Diego said. 'I'll just have a word with the nurse who's looking after her.' And she sat there and held her breath as he did what all the nursing staff did when a mother rang at night to check on their baby. She could even hear his voice in the background and Izzy held her breath as he came to the phone. 'She's settled and she's taken her bottle. You can relax, she's having a good night.'

'Thank you.'

He said goodnight, he was lovely and kind, but he was Nurse Unit Manager and that was all.

Something had changed.

Izzy just knew it.

The phone rang again and Izzy pounced on it, sure

it was Diego, only it wasn't, and she frowned at the vaguely familiar voice. 'I'm sorry to trouble you. It's just that you gave me your number. You're the only one who seemed to understand it's not as simple as just leaving…'

'Evelyn?'

'I can't go on like this.'

'Evelyn.' Izzy kept her voice calmer than she felt. 'Where are you now?'

'I'm at home. He's at the pub…' Even if she wanted to dwell on Diego or Tilia, or to just go to bed, Izzy pushed it aside and listened. So badly she wanted to tell Evelyn to get out, to just pack her bags and go, but Izzy remembered how she had rushed it last time, knew that it was good Evelyn was taking this small step, so, instead of jumping in and fixing, Izzy bit her tongue and just listened, learning fast that sometimes it was the best you could do.

'Are you okay?' Izzy was quite sure Megan wasn't. She had come and sat with her in the canteen and Izzy could tell she'd been crying, but, then, so had a lot of people.

Toby had passed away last night and both Diego and Megan, Izzy had heard from another mother, had stayed till the end.

'I've been better,' Megan admitted. 'All I put that baby through and the parents too—and for what?'

'Don't,' Izzy said, because they'd had these conversations before. Megan set impossible standards for herself, wanted to save each and every baby, and took it right to her heart when nature chose otherwise. 'Look at Genevieve!' Izzy said.

'I know.' Megan blew out a breath. 'This really got to me, though, and Diego—he doesn't normally get upset, but I guess finding out his dad's so sick...' Her voice trailed off, realising she was being indiscreet. 'I shouldn't have said that.'

'I'm not going to tell him.' Izzy felt her throat tighten. It was such a tightrope—they were all friends, all colleagues, all different things to each other. 'What's wrong with him?'

Megan screwed her eyes closed. 'Izzy, please don't.'

'Just because I've had a baby it doesn't mean my brain's softened. Nobody would tell me anything about Toby, forgetting the fact I delivered him, and now I'm not supposed to be told Diego's father's sick. I knew there was something wrong last night.'

'He probably doesn't want to worry you.'

'Well, I am worried,' Izzy said. 'Is it bad?'

Reluctantly Megan nodded but no more information was forthcoming and Izzy sat quietly for a moment with her thoughts. 'I've had an offer on the house,' Izzy said, 'but they want a quick settlement. Thirty days.'

'Ouch!' Megan said. 'Will you be able to find somewhere?'

'Probably.'

'What about your mum's?' Megan managed a smile at Izzy's reaction. 'Okay, bad idea.'

'I think I should be concentrating on Tilia, not trying to find somewhere to live.'

'There's always Diego's,' Megan teased, adding when

she saw Izzy close her eyes, 'I was joking—I know it's way too soon to even be thinking—'

'But I do,' Izzy admitted, and Megan's eyes widened.

'You hardly know each other.'

'I know that.' Izzy nodded. 'I can't stand being in the house, but I think it's best for now...' She was trying to be practical, logical, sensible. 'I don't want to force any decisions on us.' She looked at her friend. 'I'm trying to hold onto my heart here. I'm trying to just be in the now with him, but practically the day I met him I was knocked sideways. I felt it, this connection, this chemistry.' She looked at Megan, who was frowning. 'Sounds crazy, doesn't it?'

'No.' Megan swallowed and then her voice was urgent. 'Don't sell your house.' Megan, who normally was happy to sit and just listen, was practically hopping in her seat to give advice. 'Izzy, Diego's lovely and everything...' She was struggling to give the right advice, tempted to tell Izzy to turn tail and run because she'd felt that way once too and look where it had left her. Love had swept in for Megan and left a trail of devastation that all these years on she was still struggling to come to terms with—pain so real that she still woke some nights in tears, still lived with the consequences and would till the day she left the earth. 'Be careful, Izzy,' Megan said, even if wasn't the advice Izzy wanted. 'Maybe you should have some time on your own. At least, don't rush into anything with Diego—you've got Tilia to think of. Diego's father's sick, he could just up and go to Spain...' And then Megan stopped herself, saw Izzy's stunned expression and realised she had been too harsh, realised perhaps she was talking more about herself than her friend.

'Izzy, don't listen to me,' Megan begged. 'Who am I to give advice? I haven't been in a relationship in ages, I'm married to my career.' Megan swallowed. 'And I don't have a child. I'm the last person to tell you what you should be doing. Maybe speak to Jess...' She was close to tears and feeling wretched. The last thing Megan had wanted to do was project her own bitterness onto Izzy, especially at such a vulnerable time, but the last few weeks had been hell for Megan—sheer hell. Since Josh had come to work at St Piran's she was struggling to even think straight. 'Maybe you should talk to Jess,' Megan said again as her pager went off, summoning her to the children's ward. She gave her friend's hand a squeeze. 'You'll make the right choice.' She turned to leave, but there he was, right there in front of her.

'Megan...' Josh said. 'Did you get my message?'

She went to walk on, but Josh was insistent.

'Megan, we need to talk—there are things we need to discuss.' He caught her wrist and Megan looked at his hand around hers, their first physical contact in years, and she couldn't stand it because it was there, the chemistry, the reaction, her skin leaping at the memory of him, and it terrified her—it truly terrified her. She shook him off.

'There's nothing to discuss,' Megan said.

'There's plenty,' Josh insisted, and she felt herself waver, because there *was* so much to discuss but, worse, she knew that he felt her waver, knew they were still in sync. 'Not here,' Josh said, because heads in the corridor were turning.

Megan grappled for control of her mind, held onto the pain he had caused as if it were a liferaft, because if she forgot for a moment she would sink back into his charm.

And she remembered more, enough for a sneer to curl her lips.

Then she let herself remember just a little bit more, enough to force harsh words from her lips.

'Where, then, Josh?' Megan spat. 'Where should we meet?' She watched as he ran a tongue over his lips, knew then he hadn't thought this out, perhaps hadn't expected her to agree. 'There's a nice restaurant on the foreshore,' she sneered. 'Oh, but we might be seen!' she jeered. 'How about Penhally, or is that too close? Maybe you could pop over to mine...' She was blind with rage now, shaking just to stop herself from shouting. 'You're married, Josh, so, no, we can't meet. You're a married man.' If she said it again, maybe if she said it enough times, she would come to accept it. 'Which means there is absolutely nothing to discuss.'

And she remembered some more then, not all of it, because that would be too cruel to herself, but Megan remembered just enough of what she had been through to make the only sensible choice—to turn on her heel and walk quickly away.

She wasn't upset that he hadn't told her about his father.

In truth, Izzy knew he hadn't had a chance. Her dad

had been over the last two nights trying to get the spare room ready for Tilia, who had, after twelve hours of not taking a drop from the bottle, awoken from her slumber and had taken her feeds like a dream. Now on the eve of her discharge, they were scrambling to find two minutes alone.

She was sitting in the nursery, feeding Tilia her bottle, Brianna was on her break and Diego was doing Tilia's obs.

'Do you want me to come over tonight?' Diego offered. 'Help you get everything ready for tomorrow?'

'My mum's coming,' Izzy said, but right now she didn't care about her mother's reaction. 'I could cancel, tell her why perhaps…about us.'

'I think…' she sensed his reluctance '…you should wait till Tilia is no longer a patient.'

He was right, of course he was right, but though there were a million and one reasons they hadn't had any time together, Megan's words had hit home. Izzy was sure, quite sure, that Diego was pulling back—he looked terrible. Well, still absolutely gorgeous, except there were black rings under his eyes and he was more unshaven than usual and there was just this air to him that his world was heavy. And Izzy was quite sure she was a part of his problem. 'Her obs are good.' He checked Tilia's chart. 'She's put on more weight.' And then he suggested that while Tilia was sleeping she watch a video in the parents' room, but apnoea was the last thing Izzy wanted to deal with right now, she was having enough trouble remembering to breathe herself.

'I'm going to go home now.' She looked down at her

sleeping daughter, because it was easier than looking at him with tears in her eyes. She didn't want to push or question, because she didn't want to sound needy—but, hell, she felt needy.

They had made love and suddenly everything had changed.

'I'd better make sure everything's ready for the big day. I'll see you in the morning,' Izzy said, and watched him swallow. 'You can wave her off...'

'I've got a meeting tomorrow morning,' Diego said, and she couldn't mask her disappointment. She wasn't asking him to take her baby home with him, or to out them to her family, just for him to be there, even if all he could manage was professional on the day she took her daughter home, she wanted that at least.

'Can you reschedule?' She hated to nag but hated it more that he shook his head.

'I really can't.'

'There's a call for you, Diego.' Rita came over.

'Thanks.'

'The travel agent,' Rita added, and Diego wasn't sure if she'd done it deliberately, but Rita must have felt her back burning as she walked off, with the blistering look Diego gave her.

'My father,' Diego said eventually, but he could barely look her in the eyes. 'He's sick. Very sick,' he added. 'I wanted to speak to you properly—I need to go back.'

Izzy nodded and held Tilia just a little bit tighter, felt her warm weight, and it was actually Tilia who gave her strength. 'Of course you do.'

'Diego!' She could hear shouts for his attention, hear

the summons of the emergency bell, and for now the travel agent would be forgotten, but only for now. His real future was just being placed temporarily on hold.

Izzy sat there and held her baby, her world, her family, and she was sure, quite sure, that she was about to lose Diego to his.

'Thank you.' Izzy said it a hundred times or more.

To Richard, to Chris, to Rita, to all the staff that popped in to say goodbye and wish her and Tilia well, but the people that mattered most weren't there. Megan, Brianna and Diego had a 'meeting'. And though the NICU was used to babies going home, Izzy wasn't used to taking one home and wished they could have been there for this moment.

'She looks such a big girl.' Gwen was the doting grandmother now and her father carried the car seat with Tilia inside. Finally she was out of the neonatal unit and taking her baby home.

'You know I'm happy to stay over. Between your mother and I, you don't have to be on your own for a few weeks....'

Except she wanted to be alone.

Or not quite alone.

There was the one she wanted to share this moment walking towards her now, with Brianna and Megan at his side, and with a stab of realisation at her own self-ishness Izzy realised just how important their 'meeting' had been.

Diego was in a suit and he'd discarded the tie, but

Izzy knew it had been a black one. Megan was in dark grey and Brianna too.

'Hey! Looks who's going home.' Brianna snapped to happy, fussed and cooed over Tilia, and Megan gave her friend a hug, but it was more than a little awkward, almost a relief when Megan had to dash off.

Had to dash off.

Megan actually thought she might vomit.

She felt like this each and every time she had to attend one of her precious patients' funerals, but today had been worse. With Josh back in her life Megan was having enough trouble holding things together, but when even Diego had struggled through a hymn, when the one who never got too involved held the song sheet and she could see his hand shaking, this morning had been the worst of them all.

Bar one.

'Megan!' Josh caught her arm as she tried to dash past him, his face the last she needed to see now. He took in her clothes and pale cheeks, her lips so white she looked as if she might faint at any moment. 'I'm sorry...'

'Sorry?' She was close to ballistic as she shot the word out and Josh blinked.

'You've clearly just been to a funeral...'

'Perk of the job,' Megan spat. 'I get to go to lots. I get to stand there and relive it over and over.'

'Is Megan okay?' Izzy watched from a distance as her friend ran up the corridor.

'It's been a tough morning,' Diego said. 'I'll talk to

her later. You concentrate on you for now—enjoy taking Tilia home.'

'Thanks for everything,' Gwen said. 'Everyone's been marvellous.' And Izzy caught Diego's eyes and they shared a teeny private smile at her mother's choice of words.

'Thank you,' she said, and because she had hugged Brianna and Megan, she got to hug him, and then he had to go and so did Izzy, but she wished, how she wished, it was him taking them home.

CHAPTER FOURTEEN

HER parents adored Tilia.

It was, of course, a relief, but it came with a down side.

Instead of Gwen bossing and taking over and whizzing round the house doing the little jobs that were rapidly turning into big jobs, the doting grandparents sat on the sofa, cooing over their granddaughter, occasionally rising to make a drink or lunch, then it was back to admiring their granddaughter. Then when Tilia fell asleep Gwen shooed Izzy off for a sleep of her own as she headed for the door, keen to get out of the way before Henry's parents arrived, because Tilia's two sets of grandparents in the same room wasn't going to happen for a while yet.

'You're supposed to sleep when the baby does,' was Gwen's less than helpful advice.

Except Izzy couldn't.

She lay in her bed and stared at her daughter—wished her homecoming could somehow have been different, wished for so many things for her, and for herself too. Unable to settle, Izzy headed downstairs, made herself a coffee and rather listlessly flicked through her neglected post as she waited for the kettle to boil.

And it came with no ceremony no warning.

What she'd expected Izzy didn't really know. The envelope looked like any of the others from the insurance company and she just assumed there was something else they were requesting that she send. She briefly skimmed the letter, intending to read it properly later, but it wasn't a request for more information.

Instead, it was closure.

No relief washed over her. She read the letter again and stared at the cheque, and she didn't know how she felt, except it was starting to look a lot like angry. Angry at Henry for what he had done to her life, for the money that couldn't fix this, for her daughter who was without a father and for all that Izzy would have to tell her one day.

Izzy had never felt so alone.

The only person she wanted now was Diego.

Except how could she foist more of her drama on him? And, anyway, he would soon be back in Spain.

Lonely was a place she had better start to get used to.

Though she was beyond tired, when Henry's parents arrived she made them coffee and put out cake and tried small talk as Tilia slept on. In the end, Izzy gave in and brought her daughter down. She watched her mother-in-law's lips disappear when Izzy said, no, Tilia wasn't due for a feed yet and, no, she didn't need a bath.

'I'll do it,' Mrs Bailey fussed. 'You won't have to do a thing.'

'She's asleep,' Izzy pointed out, 'and a bath exhausts her.' And exhausted was all she felt when, clearly disappointed with the social skills of a tiny baby, Henry's parents left.

The house that had been so tidy looked like a bomb site; there were coffee cups and plates all over the kitchen and Izzy went to load the dishwasher but realised that she had to empty if first and right now that task seemed too big.

There were bottles to be made up, once she had sterilised them, washing to be put on—eight hours home and Izzy, who had felt so confident, who had wished for this moment, when finally she was home alone with her daughter, wanted to go back to the safety of the nursery.

She could hear Tilia waking up at completely the wrong moment, because long held-back tears were coming to the fore.

She didn't want an insurance payout, she didn't want to raise her baby alone. She wanted to have met Diego when she was who she had once been, except this was who she was now.

A mother.

Which meant even when her own heart was bleeding, she had to somehow put her grief on hold and pick up her screaming baby at the same time the phone rang and the doorbell went and she remembered that it was bin night tonight.

'She's fine,' Izzy said down the phone through gritted teeth to her mother and, holding a phone and her baby, somehow answered the front door, and there, out of his suit and in his white nursing uniform, was Diego, carrying a tray with two coffees, which he quickly put down and took from Izzy a screaming, red-faced Tilia. 'She's due for a feed,' Izzy said to Gwen. 'Babies are supposed to cry.' As she reassured her mother, Izzy glanced at Diego. She so hadn't wanted him to catch her like this. He was gorgeous amidst the chaos and started to make up bottles with his free hand far more skilfully than she could with two. The last time he had been here, her house had been spotless, ready at any given second for the real estate agent to warn her he was bringing someone round. Her intention, if Diego ever came over, had been to have Tilia asleep and the house looking fantastic. Oh, and for her to be looking pretty good too—just to show him that a baby didn't have to change things!

By the time she had hung up the phone to her mother, Diego was cooling a bottle under the tap and though pleased to see him, Izzy could hardly stand what was about to come next. She tried to make a little joke, tried to lighten the tense mood, tried to tell him in one line how she knew and understood that everything must now change.

'If you've come for torrid sex...' Izzy smiled as he came in '...you've come to the wrong house!'

'I couldn't even manage a slow one!' For the first time in days Diego grinned. 'All I want to do is sleep.'

'The perfect guy.'

She wasn't joking.

She so wasn't joking.

'I wore my uniform in case you had visitors.' He

was changing Tilia's nappy. 'I was going to say it was a house call!' He smiled down at Tilia. 'Do you think they'd have believed me?'

'I have no idea,' Izzy admitted.

'It's a good idea…' Diego seemed to ponder it for a moment. 'It's always hard when you leave NICU.'

'I would have been fine…' Izzy said, and then she paused and then she told them what she couldn't face telling her own parents yet, what she dreaded telling Henry's. 'The insurance paid.' She was so glad he didn't comment. 'The mortgage and everything,' Izzy elaborated, and Diego knew this was the very last thing she needed to deal with today. 'I just wanted to bring her home,' Izzy said. 'I just wanted one day where I can pretend it's normal for her.'

'Here.' He took the letter and folded it, threw it in the kitchen drawer as if it was a shopping list. 'Think about it later.'

But it was already there and she told Diego that and he just stood there, let her rant and rave for a while and then told her an impossible truth.

'You need to forgive him, Izzy.'

'Forgive him?' Diego was supposed to be on her side, Diego was supposed to be as angry with Henry as she was, yet he steadfastly refused to go there.

'For your daughter's sake.' Diego stood firm. 'Don't you think he'd rather be here?' Diego demanded. 'Don't you think he'd rather be here today, bringing his daughter home from the hospital, enjoying this moment? Without forgiveness you won't get peace.'

'And you know all about it, do you?'

Diego didn't answer. Instead he sat on the sofa, put his feet up on the coffee table and fed Tilia as Izzy sat there, refusing to believe it was that simple to move on.

'He's looking after her.' Diego fed Tilia her bottle. 'Maybe this is the only way he could look after you both.' He looked down at Tilia. 'You need to forgive him for this little girl's sake.' He handed her baby to her. 'You need to be able to speak to her about her father without bitterness in your voice, because you don't want her to grow up feeling it.'

'It's so hard, though.' She knew he was right, but it was *so* hard.

'Then keep working on it.' Diego was resolute. 'Fake it,' he said, 'like I told you that first day, and eventually it might even be real.'

He made it sound doable. He knelt beside her as she cradled Tilia and she couldn't imagine these past weeks without him, or rather she could and how very different they would have been!

He turned things around. His calm reason, his humour, he himself allowed rapid healing. He made her stronger, made her get there sooner, so much sooner and so much stronger that as she sat in the silence and nursed her baby, Izzy knew she could face it, could do it alone if she had to.

Thanks to Diego.

She changed Tilia, put her back into her cot and stood as she watched her daughter sleeping, and the strength of his arms around her made her able to say it.

'Your father loves you, Tilia. He's looking after you.'

And then she did what she had never done and certainly didn't want to on the day she bought her baby home. She sobbed and she cried and Tilia slept right through it, and Diego lay on the bed with her and with his help she got through another bit she had dreaded.

'You should sleep when the baby does,' Diego said, only he didn't leave her to it. Instead he took off his uniform and climbed into bed beside her. Maybe he didn't have the heart to dump her on the day her baby came home, and maybe she should just be grateful for the reprieve, but Izzy was fast realising it was better to face things and so, in the semi-dark room with his arms around her she did the next bit she was dreading and asked him about his father.

'He had a seizure. They did an MRI and he has a brain tumour—they're operating next Thursday. Izzy, I don't want to leave now, but I really feel I should go home and see him before the operation. It's just for a few days.'

'Of course you have to see him. He's your father.' And then she took a breath and made herself say it. 'Have they asked you to move home?'

There was a long silence.

'My mother asked if I could take some time and come home for a while. If he survives the surgery it will be a long rehabilitation. He won't be operating again—they expect some paralysis.' She felt the tension build in him. 'I've said I can't. The truth is, I won't. The way my father treated me, the names he called me, the taunts even now. He still goads me because I choose to nurse.' He shook his head. 'I want time with you...'

And it was the answer she wanted. It just wasn't the right one.

'You need to resolve things, Diego.'

'Flights are cheap, I can come and go. Don't worry about it, Izzy. I've been trying not to burden you with it.'

'Talk to me,' Izzy said, because she wanted more of him than he was giving.

'Okay.' He told her the truth. 'How are we supposed to get to know each other if I am in Spain? How are we supposed to make each other happy, if you are here and I am there? There's taking it slowly and then there's a place where you take it so slowly you stop.' And so then did Diego. 'We can't do this tonight. Let's not worry about it now and just try and enjoy the rest of tonight— having Tilia home…'

There was no hope of pretending a baby didn't change things because there wasn't even a crackle of sexual tension in the air. She slept like a log and actually so did Diego. And how nice it was to have her own modern matron to get up at midnight and again at four and bring her Tilia's bottle and then to put her back in her crib and to sleep again.

Diego was asleep and he rolled into Izzy, his large, warm body cradling, spooning into hers, and it was the nicest place she had ever known in her life—Tilia sleeping safely, Diego beside her, peace in her heart about Henry, summer rain rattling the windows. She had everything here in this room, only she wanted still more.

She just didn't quite know what.

Izzy found out what woke Diego at five as the most basic alarm clock stirred and she lay with him in this lovely silent place, just before waking, and Izzy closed her eyes and felt the lazy roam of his body, the natural wander of his hands before he awakened, and it wasn't sleep she wanted but him, so she pushed herself a little into him, loving the feel of a half-asleep Diego, a man following his instinctive want and her want calling him. Sex, Izzy learnt, could be peaceful and healing. She was warm and he slipped in and filled her, he was wrapped around her and deep within her, with no words needed because the air tasted of them.

She could never have imagined such peace, even as he drove in deeper, even as she throbbed in orgasm. All she wanted was peace and this every morning and the only person who could give her that was him.

'*Mierda*!' His curse woke her up an hour later, and was completely merited as it was the first time in his life he'd overslept. She drifted back to sleep as Diego dived under the shower and Izzy suddenly let out a curse of her own a few minutes later as she heard the garbage truck thumping down the street. She had to quickly find a dressing gown and race to get the bins out, then she took two coffees back to bed.

'Your razor's blunt.' He grinned as he came out of the shower and then he looked at her. 'Why is your hair wet?'

'I forgot to put the bins out last night.'

'Did you catch them?' Diego asked, and the conversation was normal and Diego looked so much better than he had last night. More than that, Izzy felt better too.

'I'll get it from everyone this morning—at least I'm only on till one,' Diego said as he hauled on his clothes.

'You'll only be a few minutes late.' Izzy grimaced as she looked at the clock, only Diego wasn't worried about the time. He drank the coffee she had made, glanced in at Tilia who was starting to stir and then went downstairs and came back with a bottle in a jug and his satchel, which looked curiously sexy over his shoulder. He mimicked nosy Rita. '*You look tired, Diego. Did you not get much sleep, Diego?* And then...' he rolled his eyes '...she'll subtly talk about the Dark Ages, when she brought her baby home from the hospital! You wait,' Diego said, and drained his coffee. 'I guarantee it.'

He didn't need to.

As he kissed her and left, Izzy lay there and tried to wrap her head around what had happened. Somehow, despite everything, last night, Tilia's first night home, *had* been wonderful, but more than that, Izzy realised, she didn't need Diego's guarantees—she was starting to find her own.

CHAPTER FIFTEEN

'THANKS for seeing me.'

She was back again, only this time she wanted to be there.

And Izzy didn't insist on the office, it was nice to just walk around the hospital grounds and not try to convince Jess everything was perfect. In fact, she rather hoped Jess would convince her that she was going out of her mind.

That she was mad, that it was absolutely ridiculous to be even considering going to Spain.

Izzy wanted logic and reason to preside, for Jess to tell her to wait twelve months, for her to tell her she was rushing in, for her to warn her to be careful.

Only when she spilled it all out, Jess didn't do that.

'I let Henry consume me,' Izzy said. 'In the end, I hardly saw my family and friends.'

'Is Diego anything like Henry?'

'No,' Izzy said. 'But as you said, people suggest you wait twelve months before making any major life decisions...'

'I offered you a theory,' Jess said, 'but as you pointed

out yourself, we don't all have the requisite twelve months to lick our wounds and heal. Life keeps coming at us, bad things, good things, wonderful things…'

'So you don't think I'm crazy to be considering going to Spain.'

'I'd think you were crazy if you were going with no consideration.' Izzy's face tightened in frustration at Jess's refusal to commit.

'Even my friends are warning me to be careful!' Izzy said, still reeling from Megan's warning. 'Megan was so…' She tried to find the right words. 'I've never seen her so upset.'

'And then she apologised,' Jess pointed out. 'Izzy, in medicine we are used to coming up with solutions.' Izzy frowned and then Jess corrected herself. 'As a doctor you are used to coming up with an answer, finding the best course of treatment, perhaps telling the patient what needs to be done. My job is different,' Jess explained. 'Of course I would love to rush in at times, but I have to ask myself, would that really help? The best I can do is allow you to explore your options—which,' she added, 'you're doing.'

'This morning,' Izzy explained, 'it was normal.' She looked at Jess. 'We could have been anywhere in the world and it wouldn't have mattered. Diego says that he doesn't want to burden me with his stuff…'

'Is it a burden?' Jess asked.

'No,' Izzy admitted. 'It's harder not knowing how he's feeling.' And Jess *was* so easy to talk to that Izzy admitted something else on her mind. 'Shouldn't I just know?' Izzy asked. 'If it's so right, what I am doing here?'

'You're looking out for you,' Jess said. 'Which shows how far you've come.' Jess gave her a smile. 'For many years, Izzy, you've had your inner voice turned off. You told yourself and others that everything was okay, when, in fact, it was far from it. Can I suggest your inner voice is coming back?'

Izzy nodded.

'You might need a little help recognising it at times, but it's there, if only you listen.'

Jess was right.

So right that there was somewhere else Izzy needed to be.

'I need to talk to Diego. I need to tell him just how much he means to me.' She stalled for a second, wondered how she could be so absolutely honest with someone if it was going to freak him out, that his girlfriend of a few weeks would drop everything and follow him to Spain with a baby in tow. 'How?'

'Maybe ring him, ask him to come over tonight.'

But she didn't mean that. 'He's at my house now,' Izzy said. 'Watching Tilia.'

'Can I ask where he thinks you are?'

'Oh, I told him I was seeing you.' Jess watched Izzy's slow reaction as her own words registered with herself. Her casual words sinking in. She had, on ringing Jess, asked Diego if he'd mind watching Tilia for an hour or so. He hadn't probed, hadn't asked why. Diego had come straight over from his half-day shift, had just accepted that this was where she wanted to be, that this was what she needed now.

'Not many people who come into my office can say that,' Jess said. 'Izzy, I think it's wonderful that you're going to talk with Diego and be honest, but can I suggest when you are telling him how you feel that you also listen? He might surprise you with what he has to say.'

'Shh!' Diego put a finger up to his lips as Izzy burst in the house. She'd practised her speech, gathering strength all the way home, and had swept into her house, ready to blurt it all out, but as she'd entered the living room Diego, lying on the sofa with Tilia on his shoulder, had halted her. 'She's nearly asleep.'

Izzy could tell from her little red face that it had been a noisy hour. There were bottles and soothers and half the contents of the nappy bag all strewn around the sofa and they sat quietly, Diego chatting low and soft in Spanish, till finally, *finally* Tilia gave in and Diego gingerly stood, taking her to her cot. Izzy had to sit, tapping her toes in nervousness, as she waited for Diego. She listened to the intercom and heard Tilia, on being laid in the cot, protest for a few minutes at being out of his arms.

Who could blame her?

'Diego.' Izzy's voice was firm when he came into the room, because if she didn't tell him now, she might never do so.

'One moment...' He flashed that lovely smile. 'I *must* eat, and make a phone call.' He picked up his phone and headed to the kitchen. 'My mother rang. I told her I would call her back as soon as I got Tilia to sleep.' He rolled his eyes, clearly not relishing the prospect.

'How is she?'

'The same,' Diego said, and he was chatting easily, slicing up bread and tomatoes as Izzy talked on.

'She wants you to come to Spain, doesn't she?'

'And as I told her, I am coming.'

She could hear him keeping his voice light, but she could see the dark smudges under his eyes, almost feel the burden he was carrying alone, and her speech went out of the window because Izzy realised it wasn't about whether she'd follow him or not—it wasn't about her, this was about Diego.

'I can understand her being upset. She knows that you need to spend some time with your father,' Izzy said. 'Not just a quick visit.'

'I have a job, I have a life here.'

'And your family is there,' Izzy said, and she watched his tongue roll in his cheek.

'Do you want pepper?' was his response, and then he changed the subject. 'I was right about Rita. All morning she spoke about bringing her daughter home from the hospital, her daughter bringing her daughter home from the hospital...' Izzy would be sneezing till next year with the amount of pepper he was shaking! 'Then she started about how the place was quiet without Tilia, how she'd love to know how she was getting on.' He looked at Izzy, a guilty smile on his face. 'Do you know what I did?'

Izzy shook her head. She didn't want to hear about

Rita, she wanted to sort out their own situation, but he did make her smile and he did make her laugh, he did make her happy, then she frowned as he continued, because in all of this he made her happy.

'She was at lunch when I left and I got a piece of A4 paper and wrote *Gone Fishing* and stuck it on her computer.'

And she could have laughed, could have just stayed happy, but Izzy was realising that wasn't quite what she wanted.

'You told me I needed to forgive Henry,' Izzy said. 'And it's the best thing I've done. You need to make peace with your father and if it means going to Spain, then that's what it means. This is something you need to sort out and I'll be okay with whatever you decide.' She took a deep breath and made herself say it. 'Whatever *we* decide.' And she was so, so wary of making demands on him, of foisting herself and her baby and all her problems onto a man who she had so recently met, so she offered a word, *we* instead of *you*, and she held that deep breath and wondered if he'd even notice.

He did.

'There's nothing to decide. We don't have to discuss it. I'm so angry with him, Izzy. Part of me doesn't even want to go for a few days, and still he goads—women's work...' He shook his head. 'You don't need this now.'

'But I do,' Izzy said. 'Because I'm a lot stronger than you think. I'm certainly stronger than I was even a few weeks ago, even since yesterday. You can tell me about things like Toby and that you've just got a call that your father is sick and how difficult that must be for you, how hard it was to get through Toby's funeral with your father so ill... We chose the wrong words, Diego—that we will last for as long as we make each other happy. Well, that's not real life. How about we will last as long as we make the world better for each other than it would be without?'

'Better?'

'Better.' Izzy nodded. 'Because I'd have got through all this and I'd have been fine, but it's been better with you. The same way you'll get through your father's illness and whatever lies ahead...'

It was a new contract, a different agreement, and Diego checked the small print.

'What do *you* want, Izzy?' Diego asked.

And she screwed her eyes closed and made herself say it.

'You,' Izzy admitted. 'And I'm sorry if it's too soon and too much and too everything, but that's how I feel.'

'Where do *you* want to be?' She peeled her eyes open just a little bit and he wasn't running out of the door and collapsing under the pressure of her honest admission— he was just standing there, smiling.

'With you,' Izzy said, and then made herself elaborate. 'And if that means going to Spain, I will. As soon as she's big enough...'

'Tilia comes first.' Diego stood firm. 'Always in this, she must come first.' And he sounded like a father and then she found out, he felt like a father. 'Always people tell me that my job will get tougher when I am a father—it annoys me, because I was there for Fernando. Always I tell them they don't know what they are talking about.' He looked right at her. 'They were right. Toby's funeral was awful, for all the reasons they are all awful, only it wasn't that my father was sick that upset me, it was how I felt about Tilia. She was a patient on my ward and I had to work, to look after her instead of be there for her...' He closed his eyes in frustration. 'Do you know what I want, Izzy?' She shook her head. 'Today, when Rita was going on, I wanted to take out my phone and show her a photo of Tilia, and I want to tell my mother when she calls and she thinks it is a baby crying at work that I am not at work—I am with my family.' She caught her breath. 'I want you and Tilia as my family.'

And good families tried to sort things out, even when the phone rang during important conversations. Diego let it continue to ring.

'Then tell her,' Izzy said.

'Tell her?' Diego checked, and Izzy nodded. 'You're sure?'

'Very,' Izzy said. 'We don't have to hide anything, we can tell people and it's up to them what they think.'

'We know,' Diego said, because they did.

It was time for the world to know the truth they had just confirmed. He pressed redial and put it on speaker and then took a deep breath as his mother answered. '*Qué pasa?*' He tipped into Spanish, chatting away to his mother, and she heard the words *bebé* and Tilia and *novia,* which Izzy knew meant girlfriend, and he occasionally rolled his eyes as his mother's voice got louder, but Diego never matched it, talking in his deep, even voice as *madre* got a little more demanding. And Izzy guessed when he used the word *prematuro* and his mother became more insistent that he was telling her it wasn't so easy—that his *familia* couldn't just pack up and come, and she stood there in wonder because he was talking to them about her, that she too was his family.

'*Te quiero.*'

He ended the most difficult call with *I love you* and when Señora Ramirez huffed, Diego grinned and said it again. '*Te quiero.*'

'*Te quiero*, Diego,' his mother admitted finally.

'Better?' Izzy asked, and after a moment he nodded. 'I said that I will be there for the operation and I have said I will come out again just as soon as I can...'

'What did she say about us?'

'That it's too fast, too soon—even though I lied.' Diego gave a bit of a sheepish grin. 'I hope you don't mind but we've been together a few months, not a few weeks.'

And then he kissed her and that made it better too.

His kiss made things better—they didn't fix, they didn't solve anything, they just made it all so much nicer.

'*Te amo*,' Diego said. 'It means I love you.'

'I thought it was *Te quiero*,' Izzy said, and she smiled because there was a lot to suddenly get used to and, oh, yes, a new language to learn too!

'*Te quiero*, what I said to my mother, does mean I love you,' Diego explained, 'but it's a different I love you. *Te amo* I save for you.' Then he kissed her again, made the world just that bit better till it was Izzy's turn to admit it.

'*Te amo.*' She spoke her first two words in Spanish to the only person who would ever hear them, to the man she had loved from the moment she had met him, to the man who, it turned out, felt the same.

And now they were a family.

EPILOGUE

You can't do it for her.

You can't change the world.

She might go back...

Diego didn't say any of those words and Izzy would love him for ever for it.

There was a trust fund for Tilia and when she was old enough and deciding her options, Izzy could tell her that her father was still supporting her.

And there was the house to fall back on as well.

A house Izzy had wanted to get rid of, a house she had hated, but now she could remember the good times there too.

And perhaps she could just sell. There were some gorgeous cottages along the coast she had considered but, as Diego had pointed out, his apartment had brilliant views and they could babyproof the balcony.

Diego was Daddy, or Papà.

They didn't ram it down anyone's throats, and certainly not to Henry's parents, but behind closed doors, when it was just they three, no one really knew that this very new couple were an established family.

And, no, Izzy couldn't change the world.

But she could help when someone wanted to change theirs.

'The washing machine jumps,' Izzy explained. 'If you put in too many towels, you'll find it halfway across the kitchen.'

'Thank you.' Evelyn stood in the hall, her face bruised and swollen, leaning on her son for support. 'We won't stay for long…'

'Stay for as long as you need,' Izzy said, and she meant it. 'Get your son through his exams, take your time…'

Many phone conversations, and a couple of sessions Izzy had arranged for Evelyn with a counsellor who specialised in these things had all helped Evelyn in her decision to take those first steps to empowerment. And on the eve of Izzy heading back to Spain, she realised why she'd chosen to keep the house.

'How long are you away for?' Evelyn asked.

'A couple of months this time around,' Izzy said. 'We're back and forth a bit. Diego's father hasn't been too well, but he's improving.' She glanced at her watch. 'I really have to go.'

And she knew, she just knew as she handed Evelyn the keys, that in six months or a year those keys would go to someone else who needed them—and Izzy wished she had a thousand keys, or a hundred thousand keys, except she didn't. She had one set and she would do her level best to use them wisely.

'How is she?' Diego asked, as Izzy climbed into the

car, and looked over at four-month-old Tilia, who was sleeping in the back.

'She's going to be fine,' Izzy said. 'She just doesn't know it yet.' She looked at Diego, his face surly as it always was as they were about to head for his home. He loved St Piran but, despite it all, he loved his family too and so, after a lot of toing and froing, they were heading for a few months in Madrid. Diego had a temporary position at his father's old hospital and Izzy, well, she wanted to practise her Spanish.

'It'll be fine.' Izzy grinned. 'Your dad's being lovely now.'

'Yes, there's nothing like a brain tumour to help you get your priorities straight in life. At least he's stopped saying I'm gay.'

That still made her laugh.

She looked at the love of her life, at a man who hadn't stuck by her—no, instead he had pushed her.

Pushed her to be the best, the happiest she could be.

To go out, to make friends, to work, to laugh, to love, to heal, and she was ticking every box.

He put a smile on her face every day and watching him scowl as Heathrow approached, and later, watching him haul the luggage off the conveyor belt when they landed in Madrid and Diego braced himself for another round of facing his demons, Izzy was more than happy to put a smile on his.

'I'd help, but I shouldn't be lifting.'

'I can manage.'

There was the stroller and another of their suitcases

whizzing past but Diego missed them and turned round, that frown on his face he got when he didn't quite get what she was saying.

'Tell him he's going to be a grandfather,' Izzy said. 'That should keep him happy.'

'A grandfather *again*,' Diego said, because at every turn, with everyone, Tilia was his, and Izzy knew a new baby wouldn't change that fact.

She knew.

'What took us so long?' Diego pulled her and Tilia into his arms, and kissed Izzy thoroughly right there in the airport, but this was Spain so no one batted an eyelid.

Six months from meeting and now two babies between them—and Izzy defied anyone to say it was way too soon.

They'd been waiting for each other all their lives.

MILLS & BOON

DECEMBER 2010 HARDBACK TITLES

ROMANCE

Naive Bride, Defiant Wife	Lynne Graham
Nicolo: The Powerful Sicilian	Sandra Marton
Stranded, Seduced...Pregnant	Kim Lawrence
Shock: One-Night Heir	Melanie Milburne
Innocent Virgin, Wild Surrender	Anne Mather
Her Last Night of Innocence	India Grey
Captured and Crowned	Janette Kenny
Buttoned-Up Secretary, British Boss	Susanne James
Surf, Sea and a Sexy Stranger	Heidi Rice
Wild Nights with her Wicked Boss	Nicola Marsh
Mistletoe and the Lost Stiletto	Liz Fielding
Rescued by his Christmas Angel	Cara Colter
Angel of Smoky Hollow	Barbara McMahon
Christmas at Candlebark Farm	Michelle Douglas
The Cinderella Bride	Barbara Wallace
Single Father, Surprise Prince!	Raye Morgan
A Christmas Knight	Kate Hardy
The Nurse Who Saved Christmas	Janice Lynn

HISTORICAL

Lady Arabella's Scandalous Marriage	Carole Mortimer
Dangerous Lord, Seductive Miss	Mary Brendan
Bound to the Barbarian	Carol Townend
Bought: The Penniless Lady	Deborah Hale

MEDICAL™

St Piran's: The Wedding of The Year	Caroline Anderson
St Piran's: Rescuing Pregnant Cinderella	Carol Marinelli
The Midwife's Christmas Miracle	Jennifer Taylor
The Doctor's Society Sweetheart	Lucy Clark

ROMANCE

The Pregnancy Shock	Lynne Graham
Falco: The Dark Guardian	Sandra Marton
One Night...Nine-Month Scandal	Sarah Morgan
The Last Kolovsky Playboy	Carol Marinelli
Doorstep Twins	Rebecca Winters
The Cowboy's Adopted Daughter	Patricia Thayer
SOS: Convenient Husband Required	Liz Fielding
Winning a Groom in 10 Dates	Cara Colter

HISTORICAL

Rake Beyond Redemption	Anne O'Brien
A Thoroughly Compromised Lady	Bronwyn Scott
In the Master's Bed	Blythe Gifford
Bought: The Penniless Lady	Deborah Hale

MEDICAL™

The Midwife and the Millionaire	Fiona McArthur
From Single Mum to Lady	Judy Campbell
Knight on the Children's Ward	Carol Marinelli
Children's Doctor, Shy Nurse	Molly Evans
Hawaiian Sunset, Dream Proposal	Joanna Neil
Rescued: Mother and Baby	Anne Fraser

ROMANCE

Hidden Mistress, Public Wife	Emma Darcy
Jordan St Claire: Dark and Dangerous	Carole Mortimer
The Forbidden Innocent	Sharon Kendrick
Bound to the Greek	Kate Hewitt
The Secretary's Scandalous Secret	Cathy Williams
Ruthless Boss, Dream Baby	Susan Stephens
Prince Voronov's Virgin	Lynn Raye Harris
Mistress, Mother...Wife?	Maggie Cox
With This Fling...	Kelly Hunter
Girls' Guide to Flirting with Danger	Kimberly Lang
Wealthy Australian, Secret Son	Margaret Way
A Winter Proposal	Lucy Gordon
His Diamond Bride	Lucy Gordon
Surprise: Outback Proposal	Jennie Adams
Juggling Briefcase & Baby	Jessica Hart
Deserted Island, Dreamy Ex!	Nicola Marsh
Rescued by the Dreamy Doc	Amy Andrews
Navy Officer to Family Man	Emily Forbes

HISTORICAL

Lady Folbroke's Delicious Deception	Christine Merrill
Breaking the Governess's Rules	Michelle Styles
Her Dark and Dangerous Lord	Anne Herries
How To Marry a Rake	Deb Marlowe

MEDICAL™

Sheikh, Children's Doctor...Husband	Meredith Webber
Six-Week Marriage Miracle	Jessica Matthews
St Piran's: Italian Surgeon, Forbidden Bride	Margaret McDonagh
The Baby Who Stole the Doctor's Heart	Dianne Drake

MILLS & BOON

JANUARY 2011 LARGE PRINT TITLES

ROMANCE

A Stormy Greek Marriage	Lynne Graham
Unworldly Secretary, Untamed Greek	Kim Lawrence
The Sabbides Secret Baby	Jacqueline Baird
The Undoing of de Luca	Kate Hewitt
Cattle Baron Needs a Bride	Margaret Way
Passionate Chef, Ice Queen Boss	Jennie Adams
Sparks Fly with Mr Mayor	Teresa Carpenter
Rescued in a Wedding Dress	Cara Colter

HISTORICAL

Vicar's Daughter to Viscount's Lady	Louise Allen
Chivalrous Rake, Scandalous Lady	Mary Brendan
The Lord's Forced Bride	Anne Herries
Wanted: Mail-Order Mistress	Deborah Hale

MEDICAL™

Dare She Date the Dreamy Doc?	Sarah Morgan
Dr Drop-Dead Gorgeous	Emily Forbes
Her Brooding Italian Surgeon	Fiona Lowe
A Father for Baby Rose	Margaret Barker
Neurosurgeon ... and Mum!	Kate Hardy
Wedding in Darling Downs	Leah Martyn